I0623316

For You to Love

Love Blossoms, Volume 2

CD Giles

Published by CD Giles, 2022.

CD Giles

Print ISBN: 979-8-9859305-0-4

eBook ISBN: 979-8-9859305-1-1

First Edition

Table of Contents

CHAPTER 1

Gabi

"Would you like to start with a drink while you wait?" asks the server.

"Yes, please. I'll take a sundown cobbler." I need this drink after the day I've had... and only my third day back in the office after my vacation. Shocker of all shockers, my boss, Adam, called me into his office this morning with the good news that I would lead a new project that several members of my team wanted. I received congratulations from everyone, except for Joseph. He has our leaders fooled that he's a team player, but everyone in the office knows the real deal. He's passive aggressive on a good day and not happy that I received an opportunity he thinks he earned.

I visibly shake off the memory of the hard stare directed at me from Joseph when our boss made the announcement. Enough already... I take a deep breath and think of happier thoughts. Jake's smile immediately comes to mind... well that and his six feet three of pure sex on a stick. Fine with a capital F doesn't begin to describe Jake and don't get me started about his six pack and green eyes. When he started a conversation with me at the bar our first night of the cruise, I damn near looked around to see if he was talking to someone else.

He's called every day since we returned from our vacation. I tried to play hard to get, but Jake broke through the wall that I erected by being super sweet and attentive. I'm not sure what I would have done without him since my best friend, Samantha, met a guy while we were waiting in line to check-in and spent practically every day with him.

Convinced that we were having a cruise fling, I sent Jake a text at the end of the cruise, thanking him for the best vacation ever. Jake walked down to my room and cleared up the confusion by letting know he wanted to see me after the cruise. I wanted to continue seeing Jake as well, but I was afraid to go for it. I smile, knowing only two more days until Jake arrives for the weekend.

Sam texted me about twenty minutes ago that she was just leaving work. I'm tacking on an extra 15 minutes since the parking situation at P6 at The Line in downtown Austin leaves even the most patient person frustrated with too few parking spots for the hottest happy hour spot in the city. With my office being two blocks over, I leisurely walked, using the time to decompress. "Thank you." I absently say as the server places the drink in front of me. I take a big sip... just what I needed. The delicious blend of fresh berries and citrus provide a perfect balance to the splash of vodka and prosecco. The stress of the day fades away as I admire the view of Town Lake from the rooftop vantage point.

I'm scrolling through the photos on my phone while I wait for Sam and stop on a picture that Jake took of us when we were parasailing. I'd never parasailed before. My fear almost kept me from trying something new. In the photo, I'm smiling from ear to ear as I point to our ship in the distance. I didn't even realize that he'd taken the picture until he sent it to me last night.

Whatever this is with Jake, I plan to try to give it a chance and live in the moment. I'm not going to lie... I'm scared out of my freaking mind right now. Sweet, nice, and a pure gentleman all come to mind when I think of Jake, but is this all an act? Is he real? Anyone can pretend to be someone that they're not for a week while on vacation. I don't have a good track record and have had one guy after another disappoint me. Why would this be different?

"Hey ladybug, what's the frown for?" asks Sam.

"Oh, don't mind me. Looking at a picture that Jake sent me from the last day on the cruise, then I immediately switched to not believing that he's for real. I'm afraid he's too good to be true. Anyone can pretend to be someone they're not for seven days."

"Hey, I hear you. I'm probably the wrong person for you to have this conversation with right now. Derek is officially ghosting me. During the cruise last week, he slipped up while talking about what he was going to do when he got home. Can you believe that he never told me where he lived? He always answered with vague responses. At first, his elusiveness agitated me, then I went with it. Once he showed his true colors, I made sure I guarded my heart and channeled my inner Rihanna. He knew what he was doing in the bedroom so *c'est la vie*. From that point forward, my alter ego made sure she took care of our sexual drought."

"Damn Sam. I'm so sorry, girl. What should we do? Remember, in high school when we took everything your then boyfriend had ever given you, drove to Galveston and used it to start a bonfire on the beach?"

Sam looks wistful as the server brings her drink and sighs. "I do... that was so gratifying. It's probably good that I can't find his ass. You and I have too much to lose to catch a case at this point in our lives."

We both laugh. Sam and I have been friends since Ms. Reed's third grade class. Paired together to help Ms. Reed after school as a reward for reading all the books on the summer reading list, we became instant friends. Sounds like we both needed this mid-week break. "How's work?"

"I bet you're not surprised. Today's my first day back and everything still got on my nerves. I'm having a hard time with re-entry. Everything that could go wrong went wrong. My major client didn't want to work with my assistant. I spent most of my day working with their preferred supplier. The client almost lost the inventory if I hadn't called in a favor. Enough about me. You know that I'm jealous, right?"

I scrunch my eyebrows together while tilting my head. What the hell is she talking about? Then Sam continues, "You still have that well-sexed look. You're damn near glowing."

I feel my face heating but decide not to respond to her comment not wanting to pile since she's dealing with Derek ghosting her. "Jake has called every day and still plans to visit this weekend. Fair warning, I may call you a few times to pull me off the ledge. I wish I could stop the inner dialogue, but I'm waiting for the next shoe to drop."

"I told you this a few times on the ship and I'll say it again. Take one day at a time. He didn't ask you to marry him. He wants to know you better. Can you do that?"

"I'm going to try. I promise I will, but this is unfamiliar territory for me. Remember what happened with the boyfriend, who shall remain unnamed? In retrospect, I had so many red flags, but never addressed them and ended up wasting two years that I'll never get back. I gave one reason after another. Some I excused as him having a bad day and other times, I summed up the issue as me just being cranky or that it was that my time of the month. I made myself a promise that I'm not doing that anymore. I will leave a relationship at the first sign that he doesn't see me for me or attempts to change me. I won't sacrifice who I am for a man. I need to remain true to myself. It may mean that I stay single for the rest of my life, but I'm ok with it."

Sam raises her glass. "Amen, sister."

CHAPTER 2

G **abi**

"Gabi, why did you send me this 911 text? Are you okay?"

"Sam, I'm freaking the fuck out. Jake will be here in less than 24 hours. I'm not sure if I'm more afraid that he'll be here tomorrow or that he won't show up."

"I can tell that you are two point four seconds away from a major meltdown. I'm actually on your side of town. Let me turn around. We'll order a pizza and open a bottle of wine."

"You're the best Sam. What would I do without you?" Just knowing that she's on her way calms me down a little.

"See you in five."

I'M LITERALLY PACING by the time Sam walks through the door. She takes one look at me. "I thought you were on the edge, but you look like you're ready to run away. Take a seat."

Sam walks into my newly renovated kitchen. I splurged on the state-of-the-art Sub-Zero side-by-side stand-alone full-size refrigerator and freezer. The gray marbled granite countertops with glass-front cabinets in a muted bluish gray pull the design together. I would normally be in the kitchen either baking cookies, banana bread, or a cake, but I'm so wound up that I was afraid I'd add baking soda when I should add only baking powder. No, I knew I had to stay away from the kitchen.

Sam filled two large glasses with red wine. God bless her. I hit the friend lottery with her. She has been there for all my major stages, to include my awkward braces and thick glasses stage. If it wasn't for contact lens, I'm pretty sure that Jake wouldn't have looked twice.

I'm about to speak when Sam holds up her hand. "Drink first."

I give her the side eye because I'd rather have my righteous meltdown. I listen to her instead and take a moment to take some deep breaths in between drinking down a healthy amount of my wine.

"Ok, Go."

"Sam, I was fine until about an hour ago. I started thinking about seeing Jake for the first time since the cruise and kept getting more and more anxious by the minute. What if he realizes he doesn't like me at all? Or what if Travis got him to realize that he should not start anything with me, especially since I'm black? Or what if he told his twin sister about me and she...?"

"You are on a roll there. I'm not sure if I should just sit here and let you keep listing all the potential scenarios (that may never happen, by the way) or demand that you finish the entire bottle of wine before I let you continue."

"Help, Sam. As you can tell, I'm really about to lose it and what makes matters worse, saying it out loud doesn't make me feel any better. These questions continue to replay over and over in my head."

"Ok, Gabi, I'm here and wait for it... I plan to spend a night. This is how I perceive it. You can tell me if I'm close or nowhere near the mark. I think that the idea of trying to explore where this goes with you and Jake has you worried that this may be a repeat of your disaster of a relationship that you had with... apologies upfront, but I'm going to say his name, Richard. How am I doing so far?" I nod, so she continues. "I am happy to see I am on track. I recommend you stay in the moment and enjoy the time that you spend together. If you need to, pretend that you're still in your bubble on the cruise. Discover where this goes."

"You're right about whatshisface. I wasted two years with him. As I reflect, I realize that I'd convinced myself that as long as I did everything that he wanted me to do by changing my wardrobe, hair and makeup that I'd become his vision of the perfect girlfriend. Even with me making all the changes, he still had an affair with his co-worker. The worst part was that she'd always been super friendly to me whenever I went to a work function. I always thought something was up with that ho. Shit–I actually thought our future included a wedding and two point three kids. I say good riddance–I put up with his sorry ass for way too long and, to top it off, he couldn't find his way to my g-spot even if I gave him a flashlight and drew him a map."

"Wow! I knew there was something about Richard I didn't like. I remember seeing you after a weekend away with him and you never appeared to be a woman who had had the best sex of her life. Like my grandma used to say, 'you never looked like you'd gotten your wig straightened.'"

I bark out a laugh. I so needed this. "You're so crazy, Sam." I'm laughing and shaking my head at the same time. Leave it to Sam to say it like it is. I calm down just with her being here. She's my ride or die. Everyone needs a friend who has your back, no matter what.

After polishing off the bottle of wine with the pizza, we settle down to watch *Different World*. Sam attended Howard University, a HBCU (historically black college or university). I love her stories about the quad and how the professors took a personal interest in helping each student succeed and thrive. "Sam, I wish sometimes that I followed you to Howard."

"We would have turned it up, but you made the right decision. If you'd gone to Howard, I wouldn't be able to brag about my best friend who graduated summa cum laude from Harvard for her undergrad and masters."

7

"With a major and minor for my undergrad, then a double major for my masters, I lost count how many times I pulled all-nighters, writing term papers, completing projects or preparing for finals. I found a good study group even though we were all super competitive. With my godfather as a dean on campus, he became my rock whenever I needed a pep talk, support, or got home sick. I thank God for the experience because it helped to prepare me for guys like Joseph."

"Is he still giving you trouble? Maybe you should go to your supervisor or HR?"

"Joseph actually plays golf on the weekends and grabs lunch regularly with our boss. They're very close. No, I think the best strategy is to stay out of his way and keep my head down."

"Promise me you will file a complaint if this escalates."

"I will." Sam glares at me like she doesn't believe me. "I will, ok? I promise." It's at that point that I let out an enormous yawn. Damn, the wine went straight to my head.

"Up with you, sleepyhead. I'm pretty tired as well. Let's call it a night."

"Goodnight, sis. Love you."

"Love you back, girly."

Jake

I immediately grab Gabi when she opens the door to her two-story condo and walk inside with her while closing the door with my foot. It's only been six days since I've seen her, but I swear each day felt like a week. Man, she's a sight for sore eyes. I can't wait another moment. I kiss her while still holding her up. She laces her fingers into my hair and kisses me like she's as glad to see me as I am to see her. I bend with her when I hear "Hi, Jake." Shit–I thought we were alone.

I slowly stand while still holding Gabi and look up to see Sam while releasing Gabi enough, so she's now standing. "Sam, sorry about that. I wasn't aware that you were here. How's your return to the real world?" I can tell my face must be beet red as a bead of sweat trails down my cheek. Whew, Sam smiles and gives me the feeling that I may have an ally with her.

"I actually took two extra days of vacation, so it's been a short week for me. I'm trying to hang onto my island vibe and determined that my co-workers will not get on my last nerve. Unfortunately, I'm already losing the battle and not looking forward to next week." She heads towards us and says, "Well, kids, I'm going to let you get started with your day. Gabi, remember what we talked about. Call me if you need anything."

I grab Gabi's hand and walk over to the sofa. Before she's able to sit down, I lift and place her in my lap. I'm pretty sure that she can tell how happy I am to be here. I'm smiling at her and marveling at how right she feels in my arms. "Good morning, gorgeous. How are you?"

"I'm good. Did you have any trouble getting here?"

I tense and debate if I should tell her. I decide to tell her the truth. I want honesty to be a foundation of our relationship. "Well, about that, I arrived Thursday evening and worked from our downtown Austin office yesterday. I didn't mention it because I didn't want you to feel obligated to make plans with me for last night. I hope that doesn't bother you."

"I'm not mad or feeling some type of way. Sam spent a night last night, which gave us an opportunity to have some much-needed girl time together."

"I could tell you had a lot going on from our talks this week. How was your week? The real story..."

Gabi takes a deep breath before starting, "My boss selected me to lead this new project. I'm stressed and excited. Leading a project will give me the challenge that I've been needing. The buzz surrounding this start-up generates more interest than normal from the partners of the firm though. One to three partners attend our strategy meetings which is unusual. They normally aren't in the weeds and happy to receive updates in our portfolio review meetings. I can't talk about it, but it's got real potential to be an app that will become a household name. I've worked hard for this opportunity and couldn't believe when my boss shared the news."

I sense that there's something that Gabi is holding back. I pause for a moment before starting, "What else aren't you telling me?"

"There's this guy, Joseph, who's on the team and he is angry that the boss didn't select him as the project lead. I've dealt with guys like him before and hate to deal with this dynamic on top of just doing my job. Ok, but enough about me."

I notice the swift change in subject. I don't enjoy hearing that there's a guy at her job giving her a hard time. There's no doubt in my mind that she's the one. I plan to take my time showing her I'm here for her in every way. I see our future, which includes me standing at the altar while she walks towards me. No, I don't enjoy knowing that there is a guy giving her a difficult time one bit. I've tucked this info away and will ask Sam for her perspective the next time that we're all together.

I hold her while we continue to catch up. I finally glance at my watch and realize that we've been sitting here for over an hour. "Are you hungry? We talked about going to Kerbey Lane for breakfast, but thought brunch at the Four Seasons would give us more options."

Gabi

Brunch at the Four Seasons on Town Lake delivers every time with a spread ranging from made to order waffles to eggs benedict. I'm now stuffed and glad that we're walking around The Domain, an outdoor mall with stores carrying designer brands. When Jake told me he would love to help me shop for a gown that I need for a Houston gala my mom chairs, I'm equal parts shocked and ecstatic.

I'm trying on my fourth dress which is my favorite so far, a pink sleeveless Prada gown with soft gathers from the neckline to my waist. The best feature, the train drapes to my left side which would make it easier to move through the crowd.

FOR YOU TO LOVE

Jake folded his six feet three-inch frame into a seat made for a large child. I'd find this funny if he wasn't watching me intensely with green eyes and a light scruff that makes me want to haul him home to have my way with him. He twirls his finger for me to turn around. I'm happy to oblige and smile from ear to ear. I'm still trying to get used to how he looks at me.

"Well, what do you think?"

"Honestly, I love it. You're like a goddess, but how do you like it?"

"I love it. This may be the one, but I have 3 more gowns to try."

"I'm not rushing you. Remember, my mom groomed me practically from birth… shopping takes as long as it takes."

I took off the gown but have been trying unsuccessfully for the past five minutes to button up this next dress. I finally give up and say in an exasperated voice, "Jake… do you mind coming here?"

"Hey." I knew he couldn't resist. He slowly pushes me all the way into the dressing room. The glint in his eye gives me a clue that the last thing he has on his mind is helping me into this dress.

When he turns me and begins kissing me, I melt right into him. It isn't in me to fight. I'm moaning softly, but remember our surroundings and step back. I glance up and notice Jake isn't even a little apologetic.

I hiss whisper, "You're supposed to be helping me."

"I am helping."

I can't help it… I giggle, backing up, and holding out my arm for him to stop.

"Ok, Gabi, I'll be good, but I can't promise that I will be later. Turn around. Wow, complicated doesn't come close to describing this dress… there must be at least twenty buttons here. You'll need help when you're home getting dressed if you decide to get this one."

"This one may go to the 'No' pile because of it, but I wanted a chance to try it first before I decided."

I see Jake looking at me through the mirror with heat in his eyes. I blush even though I should be used to his attention by now... I suspect that it's going to take me a minute.

I need to clear my throat before talking. "I realize what you mean. I need you to just unbutton it part of the way down and leave."

"Awwww, I'm being thrown out."

He makes me laugh because he says it like he's seven.

"You're too naughty for me to trust that you'll keep your hands to yourself."

"Ok, babe. Getting you naked right here, right now, would be a good idea if I thought we could get away with it. But I'm a patient man. I can wait... for now. Here you go. I'll be right outside."

It would be the last dress that I absolutely fall in love with. It's a strapless full-length gown with a black tulle overlay and fitted champagne silk full-length gown underneath. When I walk out, Jake is looking at something on his phone. He looks up and has an expression of wonder, like he's never seen me before. His expression alone confirms they made this dress for me. "Your look alone confirms this is the dress."

"I'm absolutely floored. If I didn't know better, I'd swear this dress was custom made for you."

"Thanks, Jake. Ok, I can put you out of your misery. This was the last dress. Give me a second, then we can head out."

Jake

Driving in the hill country to the Oasis restaurant always has a way of relaxing me. They built the restaurant on the side of a hill with five multi-level mega-sized decks giving breathtaking views of Lake Travis. Each level holds close to one hundred people. The server has seated us at a table with a perfect view of the sunset. "Oasis is always on my top five list for Austin. I'm amazed... it's hard to believe that it ever experienced fire damage from that lightning strike. The rebuild added to the charm and ambience."

"Yeah, and today's sunset is absolutely beautiful."

I gaze at Gabi and say, "Yeah, beautiful is how I would describe it." I'm not even ashamed that I'm not looking at the lake but at Gabi. She's beyond beautiful with light caramel skin, light brown curly hair with blond highlights. Her eyes are hazel green that appear to change colors depending on her surroundings. Seeing how she blushes just guarantees that I plan to remind her how beautiful she is to me as often as possible. I'm not sure if the other guys she's been with have been so open, but I really don't give a damn.

Gabi orders an Oasis Cooler, one of their specialty drinks made with rum and pineapple juice. I've ordered a beer on tap.

"Jake, I'm surprised how well you get around town, but then I remembered you graduated from the University of Texas at Austin. Can you believe how much the city has changed?"

"Even being part of the transformation, I'm amazed at how much it changed. Our architectural firm designed the downtown office buildings for several tech giants. Austin has rightfully earned the nickname as the *Texas Silicon Valley*."

"I'm impressed. How do you like working for a company that your grandfather started?"

"Honestly, I love it. I truly do. The only downside... folks that believe nepotism is the only reason that I have the job. I used to let it bother me, but now I ignore it. I work hard and am good at what I do."

"I'd love if you showed me the buildings that you've helped design."

I link my fingers with hers and lift them to my lips for a quick kiss. "I would love that, too. If we don't have time tomorrow, I'll take you in a couple of weeks."

"Oh, Jake, I forgot. I plan to be in Houston next weekend. You should have heard my mom when I spoke with her earlier this week. She couldn't believe when I told her I wouldn't be coming this weekend. She's used to me heading home after I've taken a trip. It's kind of our thing."

"I would have been happy to spend time with you in Houston instead."

"I didn't want to change our plans because I wanted to spend time only with you. I knew with me just coming back from vacation that my parents would expect me to devote practically all of my time with them."

"Babe, I would have understood."

I POUNCE AS SOON AS we get back to Gabi's place.

I kiss her neck and nibble my way back up to her lips. Gabi places her hands on my face and gives me the kiss that I've dreamed about all week... reality beats fantasy any day. My tongue plays with hers until I can't resist anymore. I swear every time I kiss her, it's better every time.

Gabi pulls my shirt from my khakis and places her hands on my stomach. Man, oh man, I love how her hands feel on me. I'm about to combust. Just when I'm about to ask Gabi to slow it down so I don't embarrass myself, she pulls off my shirt and begins raining kisses down my neck to my nipple. Before moving on, she closes down for a slight nip. I instantly go from a semi to rock solid.

She drags down my zipper and slips her hand inside my boxers to stroke me up and down. I let her stoke me a few more times before I flip her on the couch so she's underneath me. She has a surprised expression on her face. It's so adorable that I lean over and kiss her long and hard. I can't help but smile when I pull back to regard her. This moment will stay with me forever. Without a doubt, I love her and will, even after my last breath. I'm afraid that I'm going to say the three words that could send her running, so I kiss her neck and remain there as she purrs.

I'm determined to take my time now that I have her exactly where I want her. I lift off her denim dress and take in the sexiest pink lace bra and matching panties I've ever seen. Thank God that the bra opens from the front. My girl planned ahead. Her breasts instantly spill into my hands. I palm one, lave her other breast with my tongue, then suck her nipple into my mouth.

"Jake. Please."

I kiss her belly button and continue to my destination. I rub her clit through her panties and can tell that she's already wet for me. I grab both sides and drag them down her legs while I kiss her mound. I have her open to me and take my tongue to dip inside her. Her essence tastes better than any nectar that I've ever had. I drag my tongue up to her clit and latch on for a rhythmic suck like my life depends on it.

Gabi

I'm fucking his face and have absolutely no shame. "Jake." I moan deep within... nothing... nobody. "Aargh, I'm going to come and come hard." My back arches off the couch, but Jake stays with me. My climax goes on and on, but he doesn't stop until I've ridden the ecstasy wave. When I finally come back down to earth, I say in a sated voice, "You still have too many clothes on. Come here."

I take his boxers and pants off together while taking notice of Jake's impressive erection. His erection slaps high and thick against his abs once I pulled down his boxers. He's finally, gloriously, naked, and extremely happy to be here. I take him in hand, but he only lets me stroke him a few times before he's leaning over to grab a condom from his back pocket. He rips open the condom, rolls it on, and is plunging into me. I don't have a half second to breathe before he's pumping into me like there's no tomorrow. I'm surprised that it doesn't take me long before I'm about to come again. This man turns me on like no one else could.

His strokes are fast and deep. He's close and hitting my g-spot with precision. I can't hold back anymore.

"Shit.... oh my god!!"

Jake pumps into me like a madman. He's gripping my hips so tight that I may have bruises tomorrow, but this feels so good that I don't care.

"Gabi, I can't hold back anymore. Oh, damn!"

Jake

I came so hard that I swear I've gone to the moon and back. I just need a second to catch my breath, then I go to take care of the condom.

Gabi is on lying on top of a blanket and has one draped low at her hips. Her eyes are closed, so I'm able to take a moment to just observe her.

I lift and pull her into my side when I lay down.

"I swear I didn't plan to devour you as soon as we walked through the door." I bend down to kiss her shoulder and respond again even though I just had her. I'm in major trouble here. I'm going to have a hard time leaving her on Sunday.

CHAPTER 3

Gabi

Our drive to Houston to spend the weekend with my parents and grandparents has been uneventful. Sam and I have made this trip more times than we care to count. Since her family is out of town this weekend, Sam plans to spend the night at my parents' house. My mom said this weekend would be pretty low key since this is a rare weekend where we don't have a large family gathering.

The drive down my parents' street always gives me the impression that we're back in New Orleans with the large trees that create a canopy for cars driving through the neighborhood. Light barely filters through the thick trees. My parents' white one-story colonial with a large patio, black shutters, rocking chairs out front on one side, and a porch swing on the opposite side sits majestically.

My mother steps onto the porch as we're getting out of the car and says, "Gabi, let me see you. I can't believe that you've been home for two weeks and you're just coming home. You always come home right after a trip so that your dad can stop worrying. We need to see you. Put our eyes on you is what I like to say."

My mom gets like this where she talks so fast that I can't get in a word. She always says that it's my dad who has been worrying, but I'm pretty sure that she worries just as much if not more. Every trip goes the same way before I leave. I get a rundown on all the 'be carefuls'... 'be careful not to walk anywhere by yourself', 'be careful and watchful of your surroundings', 'be careful to never leave your drink unattended', and the list goes on. I just let her keep talking because it's useless at this point to interrupt.

"And you got some sun and plenty of rest, too." My mom yells back into the house, "Harold, you need to take me on one of those cruises like Gabi's... she looks like a new person."

I glance over to observe Sam turning her back to us. I can tell by how her shoulders move that she's laughing hysterically, especially since she knows why I look well rested. Hell, I know why I look well rested. Jake extended his weekend stay last week for a few more days. God bless that man. She better get it together, otherwise my mom is going to recognize something is up. When she turns around, I cut my eyes at her and give her the 'I'm going to kill you if you don't get it together' glare.

"Mrs. St. Claire, you're right. You could definitely benefit from a vacation like Gabi just had and to top it off, they had the best spa services onboard," says Sam.

Great save. Hopefully, my mom isn't suspicious. We walk into the house where my dad sits in his favorite chair. I walk over to my dad, who is reading an academic journal. "Hi, Dad."

"Hey sweet pea. Missed you. Your mom has been asking for the past hour if I'd heard your car drive up. How was your drive?"

"Not bad at all. We stop at our favorite stops along the way which helped to make the drive easy."

"Where are Madear and Papa? I didn't see their car when we drove up." My parents talked my mom's mother and father into living in the cottage they built for them in the backyard. The cottage resembles a house in the French Quarter. With one bedroom, living room, a modern kitchen and a small porch, the house helped my grandparents settle into living in a new city. I'm surprised they are not home.

"They had a church anniversary committee meeting. Which reminds me, I promised Mom I would get started on the shrimp etouffee. I'm glad that you and Sam arrived early in the day. Help me cut up the ingredients for dinner."

FOR YOU TO LOVE

I casually peek at my watch to make sure that we won't be late for our Top Golf kick back with Jake and his friends. We have more than an hour and a half before we need to head out. "Sure, Mom."

AS WE DRIVE TO TOP Golf while listening to *97.9 The Box*, they're playing a jamming mix of old school rap this afternoon and 2Pac's *So Many Tears* is playing. "Sam, thanks for coming with me today. Jake mentioned Travis will be there plus another friend from college, Christian, who goes by CJ. Have you been to Top Golf? I don't golf and have only been to Top Golf one other time. They have the best bar food, but I may not even eat anything."

"Gabi, breathe... you're rambling and you only ramble when you're nervous. You've already met Travis, and you said that he was nice. Why are you nervous?"

"I guess when I met Travis on the cruise, there was no pressure. It was when I thought that all Jake and I were doing was having a fling. These are his best friends... I want them to like me. Am I making sense?"

"Yes, sweetie, I understand and have a plan. Since you had a little snack at your parents, we'll get you a drink. It will help settle your nerves and will give you something to hold."

"And you promise to stay by my side the entire time?"

"Not going anywhere. I'll be so close that it will be like I'm your shadow."

NO SURPRISE, TOP GOLF lives up to its reputation of being the hot spot for millennials. With parking being scarce, we've circled the parking lot twice. We finally lucked out and parked close to the entrance. As we walk up to the hostess stand, I see Jake right away.

Jake

I notice Gabi before she walks up to the hostess stand. I'm walking towards her as I hear Travis and CJ chuckle. They were just telling me to play it cool. Fuck that. I don't want Gabi ever doubting where I stand. "Hey, babe." I pull her into me and kiss her cheek. When she shivers, I want to beat my chest even though Gabi already warned me it would be difficult to sneak away later.

I give Sam a side hug. "Hi, Sam. Good seeing you." I lead them towards Travis and CJ as I say, "Our bay should be ready in about five more minutes."

"Hi Gabi, how have you been? I hope work hasn't been too hectic," says Travis.

"It's been non-stop with project meetings and whatnot, but I guess it could have been worse. Instead of one new project, multiple initiatives could have been assigned to me when I got back from vacation."

Travis barks out a laugh. He's enthralled by Gabi. I don't blame him. Believe me, I get it. Someone nudges my shoulder. Shit, I forgot to introduce CJ. "Gabi, this is CJ. CJ, this is Gabi."

"Gabi, it's so good to meet you. I've heard nothing but good things about you and who is this gorgeous lady?" asks CJ.

"CJ, this is my best friend, Samantha, but we call her Sam."

"Hi, Samantha," CJ states giving Sam his full attention.

I'm alerted by CJ's body language that he's not only interested in Sam, but subtly making his move. Seems like Gabi notices too, because she jumps in to steer the conversation.

"CJ, Jake mentioned you met at the University of Texas Architectural program."

"Yeah, I even interned with Jake at his dad's firm."

"Oh, are you still there?" asks Gabi.

"No, I started a boutique architectural firm that specializes in eco-friendly designs," says CJ.

Saved by the bell, or rather the hostess, our bay is ready. I hold Gabi back while the others walk ahead, "I plan to get a proper kiss later."

"Is that so? You think that I'm a sure bet?"

"I'm counting on it." I place my hand on Gabi's lower back as we head in our friends' direction.

Gabi

Carefree, doesn't even describe how I'm feeling. Travis and CJ are hilarious... and the stories that CJ tells us about Jake from college are side-splitting funny. CJ, Jake, and Travis behave more like brothers than friends. I'm shocked that CJ is black and looks more like a basketball player than an architect towering six feet five. CJ's interest in Sam boosts her confidence, especially with Derek ghosting her. I will not block CJ if she shows that she's interested. I want her to be happy. She deserves it.

I'm still getting to know Jake and have probably made more than my fair share of assumptions. Jake's father now heads the architectural firm that Jake's grandfather built. If this wasn't intimidating enough, the firm is one of the top firms in the nation with a global footprint. I'm pretty sure with Jake being the heir apparent that he doesn't have a shortage of interested females vying for his attention.

Jake pulls me closer to his side, bringing me out of my reflection by tucking me into his side. Wow, with the way that he's looking at me... you'd think that we were in a private booth alone versus in a centrally located bay bustling with activity. His attention doesn't wander making me feel like I'm the only girl in the world. I can't not kiss him. I lean forward as Jake slowly bends down to meet me halfway. When our lips connect, the spark traveling down my spine never gets old. I may need Sam to run interference to have some alone time with Jake.

When Jake leans back, he asks, "Do you want to take a shot?"

"I'm not sure that I'll be able to hit the ball. If this was miniature golf, I'm your girl. I find this a little intimidating."

"Well, I'm happy to show you if you change your mind and I promise, next time we'll do miniature golf."

I love that he never tries to push me into something. When I explained my reason, I was pretty sure that he was going to talk me into taking a swing, anyway. I can think of a few guys I dated who wouldn't have dropped the topic and would have gone as far as try to guilt me into trying something that I wasn't interested in doing.

I hear CJ say, "That's it, Sam, you've nailed your stance - you're a natural. Now whack that ball like it's Derek's face." Derek, when did he get Sam talking about Derek? To my surprise, Sam not only hits the ball, but hits the second target. When she does her happy dance, CJ admires her moves. Sam has had enough guys in her life who have used sleazy pickup lines like, 'baby, if being fine was a crime, you'd be guilty as charged'. CJ gives Sam his full attention and talks to her like a normal human being.

NOW THAT THE FOOD HAS arrived, we move to the bar top table. I'm surprised that the guys aren't tripping over Sam and me to get to the food. They let us go first. My second drink arrives without me asking. Jake must have noticed that my glass was empty. Once the guys get their food, CJ starts, "since y'all just got back from vacation, name your top 5 vacations either taken or on your list to take. Ladies first."

Sam goes first, "Our cruise was top notch with each island showcasing their unique culture. I'll definitely cruise again. Number two would be Paris for its rich history and landmarks like the Eiffel Tower. In no particular order, I've always wanted to travel to Rome, Greece and Australia."

I go next, "I agree with Sam. The cruise was amazing, with the best part being that I met Jake. I went to Vancouver and Singapore with my parents when I was in high school. I'd like to go back because I didn't take the opportunity to appreciate either destination. Besides those two, I've always wanted to go to Sardinia and Portugal."

Jake begins, "We definitely need to put all of those on our list. Our cruise, hands down, was my best vacation ever." Jake pulls me in and give me a kiss on my forehead, then he continues. "We took a family trip to Toronto, then the Canadian side of Niagara Falls which included a ride on the Falls boat tour. The experience places you close to the roar and power of the Falls... absolutely, nothing like it. No surprise, I love Chicago for all the architectural history and would love to go to Dubai and Croatia one day."

Everyone says 'awwww' ribbing us since we both said the cruise as our first top five vacation. Jake remains unfazed. Sam even joins in with Travis and CJ. I'm amazed at how natural it feels to be hanging out together. I wasn't certain what to expect, but I'm happy that I came today.

Travis chose one adrenalin-packed activity after another ranging from skydiving over the Himalayas to volcano boarding in Nicaragua winning the Top Five challenge.

We stayed another hour playing round two. Jake hits the ball accurately each time hitting his intended target and looked to be winning this game, then CJ surprised them both by hitting a very challenging shot to the far end of the course. Jake sat down next to me and whispered, "Mark my words, he'll be bragging about this for at least the next month. Did you have fun?"

I snuggle in closer and say, "I did, and having a front-row seat to all the trash talk had me laughing more than I've laughed in a long time."

"Well, I'm glad that you relaxed." We watch as Travis takes the last shot then Jake, asks, "What time are you heading back to Austin tomorrow?"

"We leave around three in the afternoon after going to church then family dinner."

Jake

"Enjoy the time with your family and text me once you're ready to head home. This will alert me to be on standby in case you experience any car trouble while you're on the road. I'll be faster than waiting for roadside assistance."

I'm serious about wanting to take care of her in every way. I've picked up over the time that we've known each other, that actions speak louder than words for Gabi. Helping her if she experiences car trouble is just one small way to show her how important she is to me.

After settling our bill, Travis, CJ, and Sam walk ahead giving Gabi and me some privacy. We're quiet as we head to the exit. I saw this alcove when I went to the bathroom earlier. I take her hand and head there.

"Jake, I hope you are leading me somewhere to have your way with me."

I chuckle and say, "You know it." Once we make it to the alcove, I take my hand and place it on her hip as I pull her to me. I bend and place a light kiss on her lips before she opens to me so I can slip inside. The kiss goes on for a little longer before I stop and place my forehead on hers. Once I catch my breath, I say, "I really had a great time."

"I did too. Want to go for three for three? What are you doing next weekend?"

"I was wondering if you wouldn't mind me coming to Austin to take you out to dinner and miniature golf. Unfortunately, I need to fly out to Boston to meet a new client and discuss our ideas for their new corporate headquarters next Sunday. Any issues with us hanging out on Saturday?"

"I would love that. Jake, I had a wonderful time and Sam had fun as well. Thank you! She needed this."

"Well, I aim to please." I can tell by her blush that she's remembering all the ways that I pleased and had my wicked way with her last weekend. Good, she finds this as difficult as I do. I promised myself that the distance wouldn't be an issue and I plan to keep my word. I tuck her into my side as we head back to the exit. I see CJ above the crowd and head towards them.

I'm glad to see how well Sam, Travis and CJ all get along. This wasn't a test, but I'm happy with the outcome. Travis, CJ and I are close. They're the brothers that I never had. Between our training for the triathlon and regular basketball games, we see each other several times a week. When I suggested Top Golf, the guys thought it was a great idea, especially since CJ hadn't met Gabi after hearing me talk about her non-stop.

GABI

"Gabi, when you mentioned we were going to Top Golf, I wasn't sure what to think. I had a great time, and when CJ told me to imagine the ball was Derek's head, I hit that ball with everything that I had." Sam continues excitedly, "Talk about getting out my frustration. It felt good. Liberating."

"I had fun just watching you play. Do you think you'll want to do it again?"

"YES!" then my bestie giggles like a schoolgirl.

SITTING ON MY BENCH in my bathroom while I go through my Sunday evening pampering routine, I'm missing my mom and dad already. It's always hard to leave them. We had several rounds of goodbyes and hugs, which added another hour before we finally got in the car to head home. My mom packed enough jambalaya and shrimp etouffee to feed a family of four. She's convinced that we are not eating. I wouldn't dare tell her she's right. With our crazy schedules we barely have time for restroom breaks, let alone lunch.

I absently answer my phone and smile when I hear Jake's voice. "Hey, you called at a good time. I'm just sitting here getting ready for bed."

"How was the trip back?"

"We ran into a little traffic outside of Houston, but otherwise uneventful. Did you do anything fun today?"

"Biked 20 miles and swam five with CJ and Travis, then afterwards went over to see Jacqui's new spot. I should have known any time my twin says, 'why don't you stop by' that it's code for 'Jake, help me hang my shelves and pictures.'" Jake laughs. "I don't mind, though. She always has my favorite beer. The best part... catching up while we ate pizza afterwards."

We end our call after talking another twenty minutes. Jake could hear how tired I was. As I'm finished getting ready for bed, I muse that even though it's only about a month that we've been seeing each other, I love that Jake never texts me at night with a "u up" text message. Call me old-fashioned, but it's a turnoff whenever a guy overuses texts as his primary way of communicating. I wasn't sure what to expect from Jake with this whole long-distance thing, but he has never asked me to send "a pic" which is code for me to send a picture of my breasts or v-jay jay. Nor has he sent me a whiplash picture, which is what I call an unsolicited dick pic. My nickname for these guys is "the blind side". I don't have time. The guys in my age group are more frat boy than man. I'd rather Netflix and chill by myself, thank you very much.

I'll never forget this guy, Roger, who I'd gone on one date with. My phone dinged around eleven o'clock one night only to find he sent an unsolicited dick pic. He must have thought that it was sexy because when I saw him a few months later at an outdoor concert in Zilker

Park, he had the nerve to approach me–not embarrassed or any shame in his game–mystified why I blocked him.

CHAPTER 4

Jake
Living in downtown Houston comes with several perks. Being close to the office tops the list, plus being walking distance to the theater district and restaurants a close second.

My commute takes me less than fifteen minutes at six in the morning. Driving to an eco-friendly building that my grandfather helped to design fills me with pride. We applied and received the green building certification this year for all the energy-saving features. Bringing CJ's boutique firm to consult on all aspects of design allowed me to partner with my best friend like we used to when we were interns.

Walking by my grandfather's picture in the lobby reminds me that he's no longer with us. I miss him every day and work hard to make sure that I keep his legacy alive. I'm forever grateful that he could see the completion of our new headquarters. Even though he retired five years ago, he would come into the office a few times a week. We made a point to have lunch together on those days talking about anything and nothing at all.

Folks often assume that I became an architect because of my dad when it was my grandfather who inspired me. My grandfather would let me sit in his design sessions even when I was barely tall enough to see the top of his desk. Back then, everything that my grandfather did, appeared larger than life. He answered all of my questions and took the time to explain his decisions. I regret not telling him he was my role model. He ran his business with integrity and kept his commitments.

My grandfather taught me the value of hard work and building a stellar reputation.

CJ and Travis live their lives by the same creed which doesn't surprise me. My grandfather ingrained in me that my friends reflected me. I glance at my watch, notice that two hours have passed and see Jim, my colleague, standing in my doorway. I'd been grappling with this one design element for my Boston client all last week and had an inspiration over the weekend that I've been working to put on paper before showing my boss, Tom, for his feedback.

"Jake, how was your weekend? Did you do anything fun?" asks Jim.

"Got in some training for the triathlon yesterday by biking 20 miles and spent time in the pool. How was your weekend?"

"Our oldest turned two on Saturday, so we had a birthday party with ten kids and twenty adults. I originally wanted to have the party at home, but my wife talked me into having the party at Chuck E. Cheese. Thank goodness that she's the planner of the family. Once the kids got souped-up on sugar, it was every man for himself." Jim shivers and laughs.

I'm happy for him and Bethany. It seems like just yesterday when I attended their wedding over three years ago. I used to wonder if I would ever find that one person in the world who was my soulmate. When I went on my vacation, I didn't have "finding the one" on my To Do list, but fate played a hand in bringing Gabi and me together. I can't wait until we get married. "Sounds like a good time. Can't wait until I start a family."

"Oh no, watch out, the future 'wannabe Mrs. McAdams' headed this way."

I groan. Courtney will never give up, no matter how many ways I tell her I'm not interested. She started a year after I joined the company. To make matters worse, our fathers are fraternity brothers, so we run in the same circles. You'd think that she'd get the message by now since I've mastered dodging her advances.

"Hi Courtney," says Jim. I give him the 'really dude,' scowl. "How was your weekend?"

"Not so good," then Courtney addresses me directly, "I thought you were planning to attend the charity golf tournament on Saturday. I kept looking for you."

"Oh, something came up I couldn't avoid. Jim, I have this design that needs your input." Hopefully, Courtney gets the hint.

Jim looks at me with a 'what the hell are you talking about?' frown. He hesitates, but says, "Yeah, now's actually good. My next meeting doesn't start for fifteen minutes."

"Catch up with you later, Courtney."

"Yeah, um, of course," then as she walks away, she says in a low voice, "I guess that I'll see you later."

"Jake, that poor girl. What's wrong with you? Why won't you at least take her on a date?"

"No way, man. There are more reasons than I care to count why I would never date her. The biggest is because nothing resembling a spark or any type of chemistry exists between Courtney and me. Why don't you introduce her to one of your friends?" Jim and I aren't really what I would consider close, so I don't mention the main reason is because I'm off the market. Gabi is it for me. I knew on the cruise that I would have asked her to marry then if I knew she wouldn't think that I'd lost my mind after only knowing her for six days.

We talk about nothing, really just wasting a little time until we're sure that the coast is clear. Then Jim looks down at his watch. "I'll catch up with you later. Better head back to my office before I'm late for the meeting."

"Sounds good. Catch you later."

DISCOVERY GREEN PARK, in downtown Houston, over the years has become a true gathering destination with an ice-skating rink, restaurants, splash park for the kids, a small lake, and jogging trail that unfortunately becomes crowded depending upon the time of day. Hopefully, we found the sweet spot to complete our run by meeting an hour before the dinner crowd arrives. Today's our long run day to ensure that we stay on track with our training. I still can't believe that our triathlon is only two months away. I'm the virgin of the group since this is my first triathlon.

CJ corralled Travis into doing these with him a few years ago. I'm sure that the guys sensed I needed an outlet after losing my grandfather. Some days the grief would hit me out of the blue, especially on the days when I would pick up the phone to share an update with my grandfather, only to remember that he's no longer here.

After stretching, we run in silence for a few miles before CJ says, "I like Gabi. She's cool."

I can't allow this chance to slip by without teasing CJ. "I'm surprised that you knew any of us were there besides you and Sam." He stumbles for a second before getting his rhythm back. Travis and I laugh.

"Y'all are assholes. Not sure why you two are even my best friends."

"Of course, you do. You and I are both closet Lego geeks. Who else would have helped you build your Lego space shuttle? I can continue if you need more reminders."

"Well, whatever man. I've been meaning to tell you I like her for you. You have a problem though."

What is CJ talking about? "What problem?"

"Between me and Travis, who's going to be your best man? You can only pick one."

"He's right, Jake. Curious minds want to know."

"Shocker... but I've already solved for this."

"When did you do this? Was it during the cruise or after this weekend?" asks Travis.

"Actually, it was after my first weekend back from the cruise with Gabi."

"I told you CJ... he's a goner," says Travis.

"No, I see it too, Travis," agrees CJ.

"Can you both stop talking about me as if I'm not here?"

"We're just giving you a hard time," says CJ and Travis at the same time.

"And for the record, we're happy for you, especially after the near miss with Shelly," adds CJ.

He's right. I had a close call with Shelly, my girlfriend from my senior year of undergrad through mid-way of my master's program. I'd never been in love and concluded that it didn't exist. The decision to marry Shelly seemed logical. She was reliable, had been with me for over three years and made sense to me that this was the next step in our relationship. If it weren't for CJ and Travis talking some sense into me, I would have pulled the trigger and asked her to marry me. After a candid conversation with Shelly, she shared she didn't have deep feelings for me either but couldn't figure how to end the relationship amicably. We broke up over five years ago.

"I owe you both for helping me realize my reasons weren't a sound foundation for starting a marriage and now having met Gabi, I realize the marriage to Shelly would have been a disaster."

CHAPTER 5

G^{abi} "**I** meant to ask you last weekend, but it slipped my mind. How was your doctor's appointment?" asks Sam.

Yikes, I've been back a few months and haven't made the appointment for the tests. Leave it to Sam. Nothing gets past her with the memory of an elephant... knowing this and yet, I didn't prioritize picking up the phone to the make the damn appointment. Well, I just need to put on my big girl pants, so I just say it straight no chaser, "No, news to report yet because I haven't even had one test."

"What's really going on Gabi? Do you need me to go with you?"

I'm not sure why I haven't made the appointment. If I'm being honest, part of me is afraid of what the results may show. I could tell Sam that I've been too busy or couldn't find a time that worked. She knows that my doctor has evening hours because my doctor is her doctor. Sam recommended Dr. Robinson when I needed a doctor closer to work. "Ok, I could give you a bullshit answer, but you'd see right through it. I'm afraid... what if they find something?"

"Oh, Gabi, how about this? I'll go with you. Just give me the time and location. I'll be there. How have you been feeling since you've been back?"

"I feel fine. I've only had a few times where I'm tired, but this is usually after working forty-eight hours in three days."

"First, that's insane. Second, we need to find you a better job."

I'm about to protest when Sam shakes her head and continues. "I know that you have this five-year plan before you want to make a move to a different company. All I'm saying is I want you to take care of Gabi. When are you going to call to make your appointment?"

I take a huge breath before answering, "I promise to call tomorrow"

"Don't think that I'm not going to stop bugging you until you get this done."

"Yes, Mom... I mean Sam."

THE TESTS TAKE LESS than two hours. I shake my head, wondering why I avoided taking the tests. Once I called my doctor's office, the nurse explained each of the procedures. She shared the technician would start with the ECG, then move to the echocardiogram.

We walk out of the facility into the sun setting on a beautiful Spring Day in Austin. "Sam, what do I owe you? I truly appreciate you coming with me. Now that I've gone through the tests, I probably could have gone on my own. Kind of silly of me... they weren't bad at all."

"Hey... I was happy to be here. Now, one last hurdle. When do you have your follow-up with Dr. Robinson?"

"In three weeks unless they get a cancellation."

"I'll be there."

I just love Sam. She's my sister from another mister. She knows me well enough that I won't ask, especially after today's experience where I could have done the appointment by myself. "Thanks, Sam. Are you hungry? I'd love to treat you to dinner."

"I need to take a raincheck. I have an early flight to Chicago in the morning and still have a few things to pack. You don't owe me anything. When I get back, let me make you dinner. You're still working crazy hours because of your project."

"WHAT AN ASSHOLE!!" says Natalia, my co-worker friend. We're the only women of color in the company and have become close over the years. Nat understands the madness. As a woman of color in a corporate environment, I know that I must bring my A game every day. I perform extra research constantly to ensure that I stay apprised of the latest trends and best practices. I triple prepare by working nights and weekends. I'm well aware that I don't have the same privilege of making a mistake. No, making a mistake would be detrimental to my career.

"Can you believe he had the audacity to try to take credit for your idea?" asks Natalia.

"I hate I need to be on defense with him lurking around. I had a run in with my boss, Adam, yesterday and gave him a heads up about the idea that projects to provide exponential growth for the app. He really liked the idea of leveraging key influencers and building mystery around all the ways this app will become the next big thing. When Adam jumped in after Joseph started talking about the idea, the expression on Joseph's face was priceless. His jaw dropped, and he started stammering... shocked that Adam already knew about it."

"G, be careful around Joseph. I don't trust him... I don't trust him one bit," says Natalia.

"I will, Girl. Unfortunately, Joseph is not the first guy to undercut me or take credit for my work to get ahead." I check my watch and realize that it's already past six o'clock. Where did the time go? "I can't believe how fast the day flew by. I'm shutting down for the day. Do you have big plans this weekend?"

"My niece's christening is tomorrow which means tons of family from San Antonio and the Valley to help celebrate. We'll probably be partying way past midnight dancing to Tejano and Merengue. If you're not doing anything, swing by. Everyone would love to see you; they ask about you all the time."

"My immediate plan... go home, kick off these killer heels and have a glass of wine. Don't be mad, but I'm most likely working on Sunday to complete the updated valuation for the app."

"I worry about you Gabi. Find time to have some fun this weekend," says Natalia.

If only Natalia knew, but I'm not ready to share my Jake news yet. I need more time to see exactly where this is going. I'm trying to guard my heart because I don't want to get hurt. I hate that I'm still waiting for the other shoe to drop. Losing my identity in this relationship concerns me the most, especially my worry that being with Jake will bring with it expectations to be a certain way. Three years since my last relationship drives my trepidation. Will I even recognize any red flags? After my breakup with Richard, it took several years to get back to my authentic self. What's sad is that it wasn't until our relationship ended that I realized how much I'd changed to fit the image that he wanted.

I keep telling myself to just live in the moment, but each week makes it hard not to worry that I may be getting 'nice' Jake, not the true Jake. I've learned the hard way that guys will portray a different persona, aka what I call sending their representative.

"Don't worry about me. I'm fully aware all work and no play makes a boring Gabi. Let's just say I'm working on it." There... hopefully, I've thrown her enough for now. We've ridden down the elevator together but parked in opposite directions. I add, "Nat, tell your mom that I said hello. Oh, don't forget to bring your mom's famous churros on Monday. She promised me a few the next time you had a family gathering. Smooches."

Jake called me earlier with a heads up that he'd probably get into town late tonight since he still had to pack for his Boston trip on Sunday and he wasn't able to reschedule the late prep meeting to earlier today.

JAKE JUST CALLED TO say that he's about thirty minutes away. His timing is perfect. I've taken a long, soaking candlelit bath with my lavender bath salts. I'm on my second glass of wine and listening to my mellow mix that's now playing Adele's *Chasing Pavements* in the background. I'm well on my way to decompressing from this hellacious week.

On my way home, I stopped by La Perla to grab the burgundy silk slip nightgown that I saw in the window the other day. I love the fitted bodice but the lace webbed back sealed the deal. I debated underwear–no underwear. No underwear won out. I realized just how much I've missed Jake and can't wait to see his response to my outfit when he arrives.

Jake

The traffic leaving Houston was heavier than usual for a Friday evening leading to my frustration. I've finally parked and now walking up to Gabi's place. I'm just about to ring her doorbell when the most exquisite sight appears. Gabi stands in front of me with a smile and a short nightie with her hair gloriously loose and curly. I love it and not sure how I got this lucky. I can't even try to be cool in this moment. Ask me if I care. She takes my breath away and for a second, I need to clear my throat before I can speak. "Wow," I breathe out, "Gabi... baby."

"Are you going to ask me if I'm going to let you in?" asks Gabi.

Oh, she's being playful. Each week, she's been showing more and more of herself. I like it and can't wait until she trusts me enough to just be. "Oh, you will let me in. Over and over and over." I see her shiver and walk her back slowly into her condo. Once I'm in, I drop my overnight bag and pull her to me for a kiss that damn near takes my breath away. As I kiss her neck, I tell her, "I missed you."

"I missed you too."

I move back up to her mouth... once she opens for me, I slip my tongue inside and play with hers. I suck her tongue rhythmically while grabbing the back of her legs to wrap them around my waist. Once I place my hands on her ass, I discover that she's bare under her nightgown. Holy surprises Batman! "A woman after my heart." I murmur as I carry her upstairs to the bedroom while peppering her with kisses along the way. My heart is beating out of my chest and I'm about to burst through my jeans if I'm not careful. I'm so hard right now that I won't be able to take it as slow as I want... next time.

I cradle the back of her head while looking deeply into her eyes as I lay her on the edge of the bed. I'm hoping the love comes through even though I know she's not ready to hear those words. I get on my knees while kissing the tops of her breasts. Her lingerie is decadent. It's silky and moves over her skin like butter. I raise the bottom to see the prize that has my mouth watering. I kiss her belly button and move down to her mound.

I must not be moving fast enough because Gabi moans, "Jake, hurry."

I begin a slow drag of my tongue from her opening and can't resist licking her essence that is already dripping down her leg. I move to her clit and swipe once, which causes Gabi to damn near jump off the bed. I place my left hand on her stomach to keep her in place while I eat her like she's my last meal. Her taste absolutely drives me out of my mind.

"Jake, Jake, Jake."

"Come for me, baby." I continue to flick her clit in rapid progression and add my fingers. When I pull Gabi closer to the edge, the orgasm barrels through her. I'm rushing to take off my clothes and, in my eagerness, forget that I haven't taken off my shoes. I almost face plant on Gabi. When I notice Gabi stifling a laugh, I have to laugh too. I'm pretty sure that I look ridiculous in my boxers while struggling to take off my shoes. I was so far gone and only able to think about getting inside her. Even with this interruption, I'm rock hard. I'm finally where I wish to be, underneath Gabi with her straddling me. I thread my fingers into the back of her head and bring her to me. She looks so sexy. I pull back just to take my fill of her.

She tilts her head to the side like she's trying to analyze what's on my mind. "Jake, when... when you look at me like that." She doesn't finish her thought. Now she's kissing me and has wrapped her hand around me. I let her pump her hand up and down for a few strokes while I lay with my eyes closed, enjoying every excruciating stroke. Thank God, she puts me out of my misery and begins rolling the condom down. My eyes damn near roll in the back of my head when she lines the head of my cock at her opening and slowly takes me inside. Nothing, and I mean nothing, has ever felt this good.

I raise up so we're chest to chest, take my hand to her waist, move her up and down to keep the slow rhythm that she's established.

Gabi

If I didn't know better, I would say that we're making love right now. This slow pace is intense and so hot. I've never had this connection with another partner. Jake draws me in and begins kissing me with a rhythm that matches our sexual dance. I taste myself on his lips and drown in a sea of ecstasy... I'm kissing him as intensely as he's kissing me. Something snaps inside me, and I move my head forward while kissing him with wild abandonment. I'm so close... so close. I take my hand and begin playing with my clit. "Jake... oh Godddd!!"

"Oh god, that is so hot. I'm not... I'm not." Then Jake is groaning out my name, "Gabi."

I have no words. All I can say is "Damn."

Jake chuckles and breathes out, "Yeah, damn. I didn't even get to the good part where I took off your lingerie."

"I guess you liked it then."

He chuckles again and says, "If I liked it more, we may have been parents in nine months, even with protection. Speaking of, I'll be right back."

When he returns, he pulls me into his chest and kisses my neck, "You're about five seconds from zonking out."

"You're right. This week was on another level. I'm sorry, and I had planned to rock your world all night."

"Yeah, well, lucky for you, I don't leave until Sunday morning. Goodnight, angel."

"Goodnight, Jake."

I WAKE TO JAKE, HOLDING me tightly. Knowing that he has a flight tomorrow, I originally told him to stay home so he could get ready for the trip. Jake wouldn't hear it. He even said that he had to redeem himself by taking me to miniature golf this weekend. I'm smiling when Jake's hold on my breast becomes more of a squeeze. I can't hold back the moan.

He mumbles, "You're up."

"Yeah," and I add as a push back against him, "I see you are too."

Jake

I love waking up with Gabi. I kept my promise by letting her sleep last night. I could tell that she needed the rest. "Only for you." I lift her nightgown off while trailing my hand down to her core. I groan when I see how wet she is. I take two fingers and pump into her. I plan to do more ensuring that Gabi is ready for me. I'm a big guy and never want to hurt her. Gabi has other plans.

"Jake, now."

"Are you sure?" She nods. I reach over her nightstand; grab, open the condom and place it on at blinding speed. I slowly stroke in, then out from behind... over and over until I'm all the way inside. I need a moment. I'm already about to blow and don't want this to be over before it starts. I open my eyes when Gabi grabs my ass and pulls me into her. I got it. My woman wants it, and she wants it now.

I stroke her faster and faster while taking my hand to stroke her clit. When I think she couldn't get any wetter, she's dripping wet and squeezing me.

"Oh shit, Jake, I'm about to come... yes... yes... Jaaaaaakkkee!!"

I try to last, but her orgasm triggers mine and I'm falling over the cliff with her. Shit, you'd think by now that I would have my fill, but I'm not fooling myself, a lifetime won't even be enough. I'm so head over heels in love with Gabi that I'm having a hard time not telling right here... right now. I need to tell her first how I feel about her and that I want to be in a relationship with her, not just a weekend thing like we're filling time until something better comes along. She's it for me. Whether she realizes it, I'm no longer on the market. I'll find the right time to tell her. "I'll be right back."

WE HAD BREAKFAST AT Kerbey Lane, an Austin icon. My favorite location remains the original because of its character, as a renovated home on a street named after the restaurant. I'm ashamed to say that I always order the same thing, Kerbey Lane combo, fluffy buttermilk pancakes, eggs, bacon, sausage, and fruit. Afterwards, we mill around Zilker Park to walk off the big breakfast we ate. This isn't the first occasion that I register just how easy it is being with Gabi.

I don't even think. I stop, sit at a picnic table under a tree, and pull Gabi down onto my lap. I see the shocked expression on her face before I kiss her. I snake my arm behind her and anchor her head in the palm of my hand. I kiss her like this is our second kiss. The first kiss... I'm man enough to say that I was holding back. I smile against Gabi's mouth as she puts her arms around me. I continue to kiss her until I go from semi-hard to hard. I pull back and place my forehead against hers while I try to gather my thoughts.

"Gabi, I've been thinking," but I pause. Wait, I didn't mean to start this way. "Gabi, when I saw you in the bar on the cruise, I looked over and said, 'my God, she's gorgeous.' Then you made me laugh and that was such a breath of fresh air for me. I told myself that I would give you more time to see how good we are together. I can't believe that it's been almost three months since the cruise. The more time that I spend with you just makes me want to spend more time with you. I'd like us to be exclusive."

"Exclusive?"

"Damn, I'm really fucking this up. No, that's not what I mean... I mean yes, I want us to be exclusive, but what I'm trying to say is I'd like to be your boyfriend and I want to introduce you as my girlfriend. We don't have to change our relationship status on social media or anything like we were in high school, but..." Before I can finish, Gabi leans down, takes mercy on me and gives me a kiss that reminds me of a cozy room warmed by a fireplace on a cold winter night.

GABI

Here I was, worrying about his intentions. Watching Jake trying to express his thoughts was so cute. Exclusive, huh... I guess that I would have gone along with it since I've been saying that I want to stay in the moment, but Steve Harvey said that a man who wants to claim you, will claim you... it's just that simple. I will not lie... I'm scared, but I want to give this try.

I kissed Jake because it's the only way to express what I'm feeling at this moment. I pull back and really stare into Jake's eyes. "Are you sure?"

"I'm very serious. No doubt at all, Gabi. I wanted to ask you before we got off the ship. I would have if I thought your answer would be 'yes.'"

"We've only known each other about three months. Then tack on the distance and not living in the same city, do you think it's enough time and what about this whole interracial thing? What will people in your circle say?"

"First, regarding your time argument, I disagree... it's no different if we lived in the same city. We both have our jobs and commitments. I wouldn't expect you to spend all of your free time with me. Second, if the people in my circle have a problem with you being my girlfriend, fuck them. They won't be the friends that I thought they were."

I bite my lip as I consider everything that he's saying. "Oh Jake, you make it sound so simple. You're very convincing. Are you sure that you aren't really a lawyer instead of an architect?"

"No, not a lawyer, but I will confess that I have a few in my family. Gabi?"

He chuckles and looks at me so intensely that I take in a shuddered breath. He's looking at me with so much conviction and sincerity. If he's ready, I'm tired of holding back. I pause, take a fortifying breath and say, "Yes."

I'm engulfed in Jake's muscular arms when he takes both of his hands and laces his fingers into my hair. Having a man who knows how much I love being held with warmth and intensity while he kisses me senseless makes me feel cherished. My tongue plays with his as he slows the kiss.

As we walk back to the car holding hands, Jake says, "I promise I wasn't planning to ask you here and now, but I couldn't wait one more week."

After opening my car door and making sure that I'm all the way in, he closes the door and jogs over to the driver's side. We've been catching up on the week as he drives when I notice that we're at Main Event. This location includes the cutest indoor glow in the dark miniature golf with various themes throughout. I bust out laughing and say, "I should have known. When I told you miniature golf was more my speed, I wasn't expecting anything. You didn't have to take me here today."

"Gabi, I'll always do what I can to make you happy."

I'm so excited that I'm close to bouncing up and down. This is exactly what I needed after the week that I had. "Jake, have you been here before?" He shakes his head 'no,' while he pays. "Well, you're in for a treat. They have the best music and fun themes throughout as you go through the course."

After we pick our putters and balls, I step up to the first hole when Jake says, "Show me what you've got, St. Claire."

"Before I start, I better tell you I may have over sold this. I never said that I was good at miniature golf, just that I liked it better."

He just chuckles and shakes his head. I swear that how he looks at me will never get old. It's like he's just happy being with me, no matter what we're doing. I glance down to line up my shot. When I peek over my shoulder, I see Jake checking me out. "Like what you see McAdams?"

He looks at me with heat in his eyes that makes my lady parts take notice and my mind goes blank.

"You know it."

You know it? What did I ask him again? "Huh?"

He walks up to me, pulls me into his side, and says in my ear while dropping his voice a few octaves, "That good, huh."

"Boy, you better stop." I laugh and try to clear my head. I'm ready to go back home and finish what he's starting, but no focus, Gabi.

We're at the last hole, which is very complicated. If I can get the ball to go in with two tries, I'll tie with Jake. His sense of humor kept me laughing as we went through the course. My biggest surprise, Jake hasn't once tried to mansplain what to do, which I find refreshing. "Jake, can you help me? I really want to complete this hole in two shots. What do you think? Should I line up here?" I move over four inches and ask, "Or here?"

Jake steps behind me and once his breath hits my neck, I visibly shiver. He did that on purpose. This isn't the first time that I recognize whenever we're together the air sizzles. Hearing my friends talk about how chemistry makes everything better, I would act like I could relate to what they were saying but didn't have a clue. I now understand the difference. Whenever Jake is near, I swear the atmosphere around us pulses like a living entity.

Jake

I can't let this opportunity pass by without walking behind Gabi. I purposely say nothing at first but just stand here and breathe her in. This little seduction is going to cost me. I'm already hard and trying to rein it back. What can I say? Nothing ventured, nothing gained. I take my hand, lay it on her hip, and pull her back slightly. "Stand right here and hit the ball a little harder than you've been."

Gabi steps back further until her ass is in my lap. Damn, I wish we were somewhere more private. She innocently says, "Like this?"

"Yeah." I damn near growled. "Baby, are you sure you want to go down this path?"

She rubs her ass against my cock, making me harder. "What path?"

"Ok, just remember who started this."

She steps forward, looks over her shoulder and winks. "I plan on it."

CHAPTER 6

Jake

"**H**ey, sis! Are you in the back painting?"

"Yeah!"

As I walk to the back of my twin's new house, I see why she picked this house. The natural lighting is amazing. The previous owner added a wing and built a modern sunroom. I give my sis a kiss on the cheek, "Hey. What are you painting?"

"It's still coming together. I'm trying to recreate the waterfall that I saw while hiking last summer. The waterfall spilled into a tucked-away lagoon. The coolest part, you had to hike through a dense rainforest to get there. I plan to go back next summer."

My sister has just finished talking when she punched me in the arm. "What did I do?"

"First of all, I'm mad at you for not telling me and secondly, I'm happy for you."

"You realize that wasn't grammatically correct, don't you?"

"Stop trying to distract me, Jake. Now, tell me about her."

I rub the back of my neck then ask my sister, "What tipped you off?"

"You're my twin. It's our superpower. Did you really think that I wouldn't notice that you're working more and more from the Austin office or that you're gone most weekends?"

"J, I've been so focused on not scaring her off..." I pause as I'm trying to gather my thoughts.

"Oh. My. God. She's the one, isn't she? Like THE ONE. Am I right?"

"Yes, and I knew it right away." Once I started talking, I couldn't stop. "I met her on the cruise, and we hit it off right away. It's like the stars aligned. Her friend met a guy while they were waiting to check in, which left Gabi, I didn't tell you her name, her name is Gabrielle St. Claire. I've met no one like her. She's super smart but doesn't need to make sure that everyone in the room knows. You and I work with people who find a way to weave into every conversation that they graduated from a prestigious college–not Gabi, even though she graduated from Harvard for both her undergrad and master's degrees. It took me awhile to get this information from her. She majored and minored for her undergrad, then double majored for her master's degrees. She's very down to earth. You're going to love her as much as I do."

"I'm so thrilled for you, especially after that train wreck that you barely avoided with Shelly. I'm still baffled why the hell you thought you owed that wretched woman anything."

"She wasn't wretched, just... maybe a little closed off."

"Enough about Shelly. When do I get to meet Gabi?"

"Tomorrow. Are you free? She's in town attending a charity gala that her mom chairs."

WE DECIDE TO MEET AT The Breakfast Klub for breakfast since Gabi has a glam day at the spa to prepare for tonight's gala. The Breakfast Klub, known for their southern breakfast menu, brings patrons from all around the country. Seeing a Houston original receive national notoriety makes me proud to be a Houstonian.

FOR YOU TO LOVE

I see Gabi pulling into the parking lot, so I step out of my car. My heart pumps a little harder. This girl means everything to me, and I'm not even surprised anymore at the reaction that I have when I see her. I muse that I have never had this reaction with anyone before.

She's wearing jeans, a Harvard t-shirt and baseball cap. With her hair in a straight ponytail, she may have been trying to look casual, but she's absolutely gorgeous to me. She drives over and parks right next to me. When she steps out, I draw her into my arms and give her a quick kiss. "How was the drive over?"

I lace my fingers with hers and walk around the car so I can introduce Gabi to my sister, Jacqui.

"I ran into some traffic on 610. I bet one of the pro teams has a game today."

"I totally forgot about that. I should have told you to take the street route instead." I pull Gabi to my side as I approach Jacqui. "Jacqui, let me introduce you to my girlfr..." I'm interrupted before I can complete my sentence when they both say at the same time.

"Gabi?"

"Jacqui?"

"Oh! My! God! Jake! Really??!! This is your Gabi? We met each other last year at Connor and Cynthia's baby shower. Gabi, I've been kicking myself for not exchanging numbers. I don't normally immediately click with someone, and I did with you. I promised myself that I'd ask you for your number when I saw you again so we could stay in touch. How have you been?"

"I've been good. Fantastic actually." Then she looks at me and blushes, making me wonder which thought just ran through her mind.

The wait for seating at the Breakfast Klub could be worse, but I'm happy the line doesn't wrap around the building. Gabi and Jacqui continue to talk a mile a minute. I'm catching words here and there... "new project"... "painting" and "volunteering". I pay attention to the line as we move forward allowing them to catch up. The line actually moves faster than normal.

Watching how Gabi lights up as she's talking to Jacqui makes me happy just seeing her happy. Loving her is so easy, like breathing. There have been so many times that I've wanted to tell her "I love you." I'm trying to pace myself... the last thing that I want her to think is I'm coming on too strong or moving too fast. It's taken all my life to find her; I don't plan to fuck this up by scaring her away now.

The server calls our names finally, Gabi grabs my hand as she and Jacqui continue to talk like lifelong friends who haven't seen each other in forever. After placing our orders, Jacqui finally looks over and says, "I still can't believe how small this world is. Gabi, tell me how you met. Jake said that it was while you were on the cruise both taking a much-needed vacation."

"My vacation started off kind of crappy. My friend ended up meeting this guy while we were waiting to check-in."

"No way... are you serious? You mean that she actually abandoned you before your cruise even started. What did you do? Did you say anything to her? I would have been pissed," says Jacqui with an emphasis on the *d*.

"No, don't be mad at Sam. I'd planned to work at least half the time while I was on the ship. Where was I? Oh yeah, I'd worked a full day the first day," Jacqui gives her a shocked expression, "Shocker, right? Who works an eight-hour day on their first day of vacation? Anyway, I needed a drink like nobody's business. There's a bar in the middle of the ship that all the bloggers rave about since it's on hydraulics and elevates the bar six stories in the air. I ended up sitting next to Jake and when the bar got stuck for over thirty minutes, we talked non-stop."

I jump in "I knew that there was something special about Gabi. I could not leave it up to chance that we'd run into each other sometime over the next seven days... the ship had over five thousand passengers and I knew the odds were not in my favor." I shudder just thinking what would have happened if I'd left it up to chance. I wouldn't be sitting here introducing Gabi to Jacqui. My life would be very different. I'm a happy man because I pushed for the first date. "I asked her out on a date for the very next day. We spent the entire cruise together."

Jacqui says, "Awwww, that's sweet." Then she adds, "Gabi, if he ever gives you a hard time, just call me. I'll straighten him out for you."

I just shake my head and love that Jacqui really likes Gabi. I hadn't contemplated if Jacqui would like Gabi. I'd hoped that over time they would get closer. If Gabi says 'yes' when I ask her to marry me, she'll be my wife one day. Being twins, Jacqui and I have often joked that whoever becomes our significant other, they will have to understand and accept that we're a package deal.

Our food arrives. I love Gabi doesn't shy away from her Creole heritage. She ordered the shrimp and grits with biscuits plate which looks delicious, by the way. I make a mental note to order it next time we come. I'm having the French toast plate which doesn't disappoint, and Jacqui dived into her pancakes and eggs.

"Gabi, Jake tells me you're going to a gala tonight."

"Yes. STEM Society sponsors the gala. My mom heads the charity as this year's board president. Their mission introduces at-risk African American students to science, technology, engineering, and math. They fundraise to offer scholarships, STEM summer camps, after-school programs, and college field trips. Each year they give five students in the city a twenty thousand scholarship to the school of their choice."

"Wow! That's an amazing charity," exclaims Jacqui.

Jacqui and Gabi have been talking non-stop. It's like they're lifelong friends. I'm smiling as I try to jump into the conversation. "Gabi, I agree with Jacqui." I ask, "When did your mom become involved with the charity?"

"She discovered this charity two years after we moved to Houston after Hurricane Katrina. My dad often says this charity helped her grow roots here. My mom and grandmother both wanted to go back home.

There's truly nothing like New Orleans with its rich Creole history and down-home food. My dad convinced her that going back wouldn't be the same since so much had changed. Many of their friends are now scattered all over the United States," says Gabi.

"Gosh, babe, I remember you talking about this when we were on the cruise. I'm just understanding how disruptive the hurricane has been in your life." I take her hand and hold on tight. I hope she can sense the sincerity in what I'm saying. I try to lighten the mood. "Are you wearing the dress that you picked that first weekend when I was in Austin?"

She speaks, but not before I notice her blush. I bet she's remembering like I am how much fun we had when I was helping her in and out of one dress. "Yes, and the best part is I had the accessories that I needed in my closet."

"Gabi, what type of dress are you wearing tonight?" asks Jacqui.

"First, your brother was a trooper. I think I tried on at least seven dresses and, of course, the last dress I tried on is the one that I positively fell in love with. The strapless champagne dress has a black tulle overlay with a silk full-length gown underneath. Jacqui, I feel like a super model especially since the gown looks couture." says Gabi.

"Wow! You've got to send me a picture. It sounds gorgeous. Next month, I'm going to the MD Anderson gala and need to find a dress. I'll keep you posted if I'll need to make a shopping trip to Austin." states Jacqui then she adds, "I still can't believe that you're my brother's Gabi. What are the odds?" asks Jacqui.

GABI

I shake my head in amazement. "It's crazy how small this world truly is." I peek down at my watch. Two hours have passed in a blur. "I hate to eat and run, but I'm going to be late if I don't leave now for my spa appointment."

Jake settles the bill and leaves a generous tip. He may not be aware, but this is a major turn on for me. One of my pet peeves is a date who justifies why they give little or no tip. He pulls me to his side and says, "Let's get you on your way."

Once we reach our cars, I step away and give Jacqui a big hug, "Jacqui, it was so good seeing you and now we've exchanged numbers so we can stay in touch."

"Don't forget to send me a picture of the dress. Mark my words... you're going to be the belle of the ball," says Jacqui.

I turn back to Jake, suddenly very shy. Should I kiss him on the lips, on the cheek or not all. Jake must understand my dilemma because he decides for me and gives me a goodbye kiss that will be enough to hold me over until I see him next week.

When the kiss is over, I slowly open my eyes and forget where I am for a moment. Thank God Jake is still holding me because my legs are a little shaky. He's looking down at me and chuckles while I whisper, "Wow."

"Me too, sweetheart, me too."

I snap my head in Jacqui's direction to find she is already in the car and didn't witness the kiss that transported me to another dimension. "I guess I better go."

"Drive carefully and I'll talk to you tomorrow before you head back."

"Bye Jake."

Jake

Jacqui and I are each in our own thoughts when she says, "I'm happy for you. You did good, Jake. Gabi brings something out in you I've never seen before."

"She does?" I glance over and wait patiently as she's tries to find the right words. My curiosity gets the best of me and I demand, "Well, don't keep me in suspense."

Oh, I see the gleam in her eyes. She's debating if she's going to tell me now or make me suffer. I squint my eyes at her, telling her without saying, you're going to be sorry if you don't put me out of my misery. Finally, she speaks, "This may sound a little weird, so give me a minute as I try to explain. You seem more grounded, or maybe... it's more like you've settled down and aren't so antsy. If I'm being honest, you've worried me. I knew you weren't in a good place, but I had no clue what to do about it. We're both still reeling from losing grandpa but you and him had a special bond. I'm glad to see my old Jakey back."

I should have known that Jacqui would have picked up on my restlessness. Whenever I've been around my family, I tried my best to appear the same and not to show how much my granddad's passing affected me. Before going on the cruise, I felt lost like walking in a forest trying to find my way back to town, but each path took me by the same tree stump, only to realize that I was back where I started.

"Jacqui, Gabi is the one. I'd ask her to marry me right now if I didn't think that I'd run her away. I love her with every bone in my body. It's no secret that I've dated off and on over the years. None of those women even come close to Gabi. She's like my missing puzzle piece and I knew it as soon as I touched her hand."

"You're right in taking it slow. If a guy that I'd only known for three months asked me to marry him, I'd wonder what the hell. My advice to you is to give it more time. By the way, she loves you too."

"You think so?"

"Yeah, I know so. A woman can recognize when another woman is in love."

Gabi

The gala's black and gold theme transports me back to the Harlem Renaissance. Even the valets are wearing black tailed tuxes. Astorian's main vestibule in Houston fits the theme so well that if I hadn't already been to the Astorian a few times, I'd think that the owners redecorated for this occasion. Black pillars adorned with gold sconces throughout pave my way as I walk towards the ballroom with five huge ten-tier chandeliers lighting my path.

As soon as I enter the ballroom, I find my mom and dad talking to members from the board. I kiss both as I say, "Hi, Mom. Hi, Dad. You've outdone yourself with this year's gala. Mom, love the dress. You're absolutely beautiful."

"Thanks sweetie, and you're like a princess ready for her ball. It's a shame that you showed up alone. Ms. Jackson's son is single, and I have it on good authority that he came alone."

I smile when she mentions Ms. Jackson's son, Bryce. They're from back home, so I've known Bryce since we were four. We have never thought of each other as anything but friends, besides I don't have the equipment that Bryce wants. It's not up to me to "out" him to my mom and his. "Mom, I love Bryce like a brother. It would be good to catch up though. I haven't seen him since Thanksgiving."

"Sounds good. I saw him heading to the bar just now."

"Before I head over, how's the fundraiser going so far?"

"We're having a great night even before the silent auction. We've raised close to one hundred thousand dollars so far. Even though, you've just returned from vacation, I'd recommend bidding on the one-week stay at an oceanfront villa off the coast of Tortola in the British Virgin Islands. One of our board members owns the villa. I predict this will be the number one item tonight. He added a 40-picture digital photo album of the villa with breathtaking sunrise and sunset views."

"Sounds like a beautiful location. I may bid on some other items as well. Do you need anything, Mom?"

"We're good. Go have a great night."

"Now, that I can do, love you, Mom." Well, speak of the devil. Bryce walks towards me with two drinks in his hands. He's going to make some man a great husband one day. He's a little over six feet tall, built like a professional football player with chocolate brown skin, and a low-cut beard that rivals any male model. "Hey buddy... you're wearing that tux like nobody's business." He hands me my go-to drink pineapple with coconut rum. "Thanks."

He bends and gives me a kiss on the cheek. "How have you been? You look gorgeous, by the way."

We walk towards the room where the silent auction is being held. "I've been good, very good, actually. When we talked at Thanksgiving, you shared you were going to tell your mom that your best friend, Malcolm, was actually your partner. My mom just tried to set us up."

"I'd planned to tell her before Christmas, then my grandma fell and broke her hip. I didn't want to pile on. My mom's had enough on her plate."

"Well, the offer still stands. I can be your support buddy when you tell them. I'm happy to be there for you. Your mom actually may surprise you and has already figured it out."

"You're probably right."

CHAPTER 7

J**ake**

    Gabi and I meet after work giving me a glimpse into how our life would be when I permanently move to Austin. The current manager retires from the firm at the end of the year, giving us time to transition operations to me. When my dad approached me with the opportunity, I jumped at the chance. Leaving Gabi each week has been getting harder and harder. By accepting the Austin role, we can spend more time together, even if it's only grabbing the occasional lunch during the week.

For dinner, we decided on Suerte, an upscale Mexican restaurant in East Austin, known for their quesadillas, homemade tortillas and brisket tacos. Taking a sip of my beer, I muse how fate played a hand in bringing Gabi into my orbit. She updates me on the current project. Her eyes sparkle as she explains the latest development where the mastermind of the app wants to launch during the mega tech conference in a few months.

"Jake, I'm telling you... this app is a game changer. Our sessions need to shift from valuation to creative ways to generate buzz. I'm excited and stressed at the same time."

I grab her hand. "You've got this and don't let anyone tell you otherwise. You've got amazing ideas and are going to do a phenomenal job. Now, how's Joseph? Is he still an issue?"

Before she can answer, our food arrives. "Your brisket tacos make me wish that I ordered those instead. But to answer your question, no trouble from Joseph. The company gave him a short-term assignment in San Francisco providing onsite support to a new start-up preparing for their IPO."

"I'm glad to hear that Joseph will be out of your hair for an extended period. If things change, you'll let me know?"

"Yes, I will."

"Would you like a taco?"

"Sure, would you like some of my quesadilla?"

"You bet! Are you excited about winning the one-week stay at the villa in the Virgin Islands from the silent auction?"

"I still can't believe that I won. My mom and dad have their thirty-year wedding anniversary coming up in nine months. I plan to gift the trip to them. Being workaholics, they rarely take a vacation."

"They're going to love it and sounds like it's well deserved." Gabi takes a bite of the brisket taco with a moan that goes straight to my dick. I grab the edge of the table so hard that my knuckles turn white. When she licks her lips, I whisper, "have mercy". If I didn't know better, I'd swear that she's doing this on purpose.

I open my eyes to see her raise an eyebrow and ask, "How you doing over there, Jake?" So, she is doing this on purpose.

"Not doing too well, Gabi, actually it's pretty hard over here."

"Is it now?"

SINCE WE DROVE IN SEPARATE cars, I'm following Gabi to her place with a hard on that could break bricks. Throughout our dinner, Gabi would do one seductive thing after another. When she took her foot and brought it between my legs, I wanted to take her right there on the table. If it wasn't for the possibility of having an indecent exposure charge, I just might have done it.

FOR YOU TO LOVE

Gabi parks before I do and is out of her car, swinging her hips proudly left to right with her head held high as she walks towards her door. Watching her hips swing focus my attention on her like a beacon of light on a lighthouse does to guide boats back to the harbor. I'm a man hanging on a by a thread. She looks over her shoulder, giving me a seductive look with bedroom eyes that rachets my need for her to another level.

Once she opens the door, I have my hands on her hips, hurrying her into the condo. I close the door with my foot. Pull her back into my front so she can tell just how hard I am for her. "Do you see how much I want you?" I kiss her neck as she shivers.

"Good to see that I've still got it. What are you going to do about it?"

"I'd rather show you." I spin her so she's against the wall and lean down to kiss her. She opens for me as I slip my tongue inside. I grab her tongue, begin sucking as I palm her breast.

Gabi trails her hand down the front of my slacks as she traces the outline of my dick. "Jake, hurry."

She literally takes matters into her own hands, unzips my pants, begins stroking me with her hand while dropping to her knees. When she takes me in her mouth, I have to slap a hand against the wall. "Oh, Gabi, that... that, oh baby." When she cups my balls in her hand while taking me deeper, I pump slightly. She has me so turned on from dinner that I'm already about to come. No, not yet she's first... always first.

I pull her up as she exclaims, "Jake!"

I'm too consumed and singularly focused... I need her now. Good heavens, she has another front clasp on her bra. In my urgency, I damn near break the front clasp before her breasts spill out. I'm so far gone. I can't figure out which one I want to suck first. I draw her left breast into my mouth while taking the nipple of her other breast and roll between my fingers. I alternate while trailing my hand down and raising her skirt until it's bunched around her waist. "Are you wet, Gabi?"

She breathes out, "Yes."

She's dripping wet and I have to taste her. I pull down her thong while dropping to my knees. I take a slow swipe, letting her essence coat my tongue. When I get to her clit, I make rapid flicks that send her trembling.

"Jake, I'm... I'm... oh commmming!"

I raise up while pulling the condom out of my pocket. Gabi is as desperate as I am, helps me to roll the condom, and wraps her legs around me. I impale her and begin pumping her long, hard. "Gabi, you feel so damn good."

"Faster Jake! Faster!"

I grab her hips and develop a rhythm where I'm pumping fast with deep strokes. "I'm close, but I need you with me." I reach down and stroke her clit while I continue fast strokes. She grips my dick with her walls... she's close.

"Jake... Jake... Jake," as she climaxes.

I'm out of my mind as my release slams into me like a freight train. "Gabiiiiiiiiiiii!" When I finally come down, I kiss her on the tip of her nose and whisper the one thing that is beating like a drum waiting to burst out of my chest, "I love you." Shit, I should have led up to saying that. I hold my breath and slowly look into Gabi's eyes to see them glistening with unshed tears.

"I love you, too."

I release a breath that I'm holding and kiss her deeply. I really thought that I'd messed up there for a second. "Thank fuck."

Gabi

Even though we made love last night before falling asleep, I want him now. I've never been insatiable before, but with Jake I'm discovering a new side of myself. Just when I'm about to make it known that I'm up, Jake's hand gently squeezes my breast, kisses my shoulder, and says, "Good morning."

I whisper, "Good morning," as I turn, kiss his chest while urgently placing my hand around his swollen member. I stroke slowly up and down; up and down. Jake lays back, enjoying my ministrations as he gets harder and moves with me.

"Gabi, baby... feels... oh... I need."

I reach over and grab the condom off the nightstand. Roll it down and straddle him while slowly taking every single inch of him. I love torturing both of us as I lift almost all the way up before starting over. I slowly pick up the pace but enjoy seeing how Jake is trying to hold back... digging his fingers into my thighs. I close my eyes and enjoy this exquisite feeling of connecting with the man that I love. Jake takes his thumb and plays with my clit. "Oh, Jake, that... good, so good, so damn good. I can't... I can't."

"Don't hold back, Gabi. Give it to me. I'm so close but you first."

My orgasm starts at my feet and races through my body. "Oh, yes... yessssss!"

Jake flips me, takes my right thigh, hooks it over his arm and grinds deep, slow and long strokes. When he opens me wider, he hits my g-spot, which triggers another orgasm. "Jaaaaaakkkkkeeee!"

He growls deep from the depths of his soul when he says, "Gabi."

The room is silent except for our heavy breathing. "I have no words, Jake. Just when I think it couldn't get better, you surprise me."

He smiles against my shoulder. "It's all you, Ms. St. Claire. I'm very motivated and single-minded with you." He kisses my shoulder as he rises. "I'll be right back."

CHAPTER 8

Gabi

While washing dishes, I'm absentmindedly humming Aaliyah's *4 Page Letter* that's playing in the background as I reflect on the last four months with Jake. We've gotten into a simple rhythm where we see each other every weekend. Unfortunately, Jake normally drives to Austin, since my work schedule has made it difficult to get away over the past few weeks. I take a shuddered breath, realizing that I'm happy but still afraid... I can't stop myself from worrying about the unknown. Like what if Jake turns out to be like Richard or Jake's ex-fiancé, Shelly, decides that she wants Jake back and he's open to seeing if their relationship can be more now that they are older... wiser.

Jake walks back into the house wearing a burnt orange University of Texas t-shirt with black jogging pants holding two steaks and baked potatoes that's he's grilled on the gas grill that he purchased. I chuckle as I recall his shock that I didn't have a gas grill in my backyard. My argument was sound. What single, twenty-eight-year-old woman did he know who owned a gas grill... really?

I'm wearing an orange halter dress with purple and magenta colors weaved throughout the pattern, and the best part is I don't have on any makeup today. He bends to kiss my shoulder, turns me around, and now my hands are dripping with soap. I protest weakly, loving how affectionate he is. "You're going to get wet."

As he kisses the spot on my neck that he's discovered drives me absolutely insane, Jake murmurs, "I love when you get me wet." Jake lifts his head murmurs "dinner can wait" and pulls me closer for a kiss that is packed with so much heat that I forget about dinner.... what dinner? He continues to kiss me deeply. I'm unable to hold back my moan when he grabs my tongue and sucks with just the right amount of pull that tugs down to my lady parts. I'm melting more into his embrace like a moth to his flame.

Jake becomes harder and harder with each passing moment. I'm vaguely aware that he's moving us, I don't even care as long as it means we're both naked and making the most of every minute that we have together.

Jake

Gabi revs me up like nobody's business. I've gotten used to being semi-hard any time I'm in her presence. Voracious doesn't even explain how deep my appetite for Gabi goes and now that we've told each other "I Love You," I want her more, if that is even possible. I want her to understand how much I treasure her and how precious she is to me. She never has to worry that I would ever break her heart.

The bedroom is too far away but the kitchen island will do. I gently lift Gabi up and lay her back.

"Jake, hurry... I want you now."

"Patience baby, I need to taste you first. I'm not ashamed to say that it's practically all I've thought about since I left you last weekend." I slowly trail my hand up her dress and take a finger to tease her before removing her boy shorts while my other hand reaches up to pinch her nipple through her dress.

"Dammit, Jake, if you don't stop playing," she pants while I remove her underwear.

I lift her dress and notice that she waxed. I have to confirm, "Is this for me?"

She says, "Yes, what are you...," but whatever sassy retort she was going to make becomes a deep soul-rendering moan when I take my nose, glide up from her opening and suck her clit hard before eating her like this is our first time and I have something to prove. I alternate between stiffing my tongue to fuck her opening and flicking her clit rapidly while taking two fingers to bring as much pleasure to her as possible. I'm getting so turned on right now. Can't wait until I'm so deep inside that I discover something new that turns Gabi on even more than she already is.

"Jake... oh Jake... oh... oh," then her back is arching off the island as her orgasm slams into her. I remove the condom from my back pocket before dropping my pants, putting on the condom and pushing into her with one stroke.

"Gabi, look at me." I'm so far gone that I don't even recognize my voice.

She opens her eyes and I see the love. It's like we're in on our own love cocoon. I grab her hips while I long stroke her repeatedly. Gabi's next orgasm triggers mine, but I keep pumping into her as she rides the pleasure wave.

It takes time for my brain to work. "Damn Gabi. I promise I didn't walk into here to... to..."

"Put me in a sex coma?"

I chuckle, "Yes, that." I give her one last kiss, gently pull out while holding the condom with one-hand and helping Gabi down from the island. "I'll be right back."

AFTER GETTING CLEANED up, we ate dinner and now sit on her couch as we listen to jazz while drinking a glass of the red wine that I introduced her on the cruise. She's been more quiet than normal since she sat down. I pull her more into my side and kiss her temple while saying, "A penny for your thoughts. Is everything ok?"

At first, she says nothing then she turns so she can look at me. I see worry in her gaze, "Baby, whatever it is, you can tell me. You can tell me anything."

"Jake, I just hope when I tell you, you won't be mad that I didn't tell you earlier, or think I was trying to keep something from you."

I take her hands because she is wringing them and making herself more upset. "How about you start wherever you'd like?"

"First, I wanted to tell you earlier this week. I decided talking face-to-face would be better." She takes a deep breath, "Okay, well you're aware how busy this project has had me, working long hours and barely getting a lunch."

I nod, not wanting to interrupt her. I want to make this as easy as possible for her to explain what's bothering her. Gabi continues, "I've had a few tests for my heart that have come back inconclusive. The doctor wants me to have one last test."

"Oh, babe. Is everything okay? Whatever it is, we'll face it together."

"I have my doctor's appointment on Monday. Sam was originally going to go with me. Unfortunately, she called this morning with the news that she's stuck in Chicago for at least the next ten days due to construction delays on her project. Are you sure, Jake? This is a big ask. No new boyfriend wants to handle a potential medical crisis." Gabi takes a gigantic sigh and adds, "I haven't told my parents yet because I want to wait until I have more information and don't want them to worry unnecessarily."

I lift Gabi so she's in my lap and smile when she lays her head on my shoulder. I rub my hand up and down her back before starting, "Babe, I remember a few times during the cruise that you would get quiet and stare, but not look at anything in particular. I realized something was on your mind then and wanted to ask but didn't want to pry. Besides, at that point, I was trying hard to figure exactly how to keep seeing you after the cruise." Gabi laughs so I continue, "Yeah, I was already in love with you if I'm being honest."

"Jake, no... you'd only just met me. I'm pretty sure that it was more like a really strong like or lust."

"If you don't believe me, you can ask Travis. I should try to keep my man card, but I don't want to be like that with you. You have my heart, Gabi St. Claire."

She looks up and gives me a simple kiss, but I kiss her softly as what she's shared rocks me to my core. God wouldn't be so cruel to bring my soulmate into my life then limit the time we have. A vision of Gabi's swollen belly with my child slams into my thoughts. I want everything with her.

I stand with her in my arms and walk to her bedroom. I want to hold her properly. I undress her and find her favorite nightgown, then undress while keeping on my navy silk boxers. I lay on my back so she can lie in the crook of my neck. When she drags her leg up against mine, my dick twitches, but that's not what she needs right now.

We're both quiet for a while when I say, "Gabi, thanks for telling me. You shouldn't go through this by yourself. I'm happy you have Sam. You and Sam remind me of Travis, CJ, and me. She's a great friend. I love you and will always be here for you."

"I love you too, Jake. I appreciate you taking the news so well. I was afraid that you would think that I purposely withheld this information from you."

"No, babe, never."

Gabi

We had a great weekend. I was going stir crazy sitting around Sunday, so Jake suggested canoeing on Town Lake in downtown Austin taking advantage of the springtime temperatures. I had the bonus of checking out Jake's muscles. He caught me checking him out at one point, winked at me and flexed on purpose, making me laugh.

Jake grabs my hand as we wait for the nurse to call me back for my appointment. My leg keeps jumping nervously, so much so that I need to take my hand to hold it down. Jake must notice as well because he leans over and says, "Hey, everything is going to be fine. We've got this."

"Oh, we do?" I pause for a moment then whisper, "Thanks for coming." I'm finally put out of my misery when they call my name. We stand together as I take a shaky breath and follow the nurse.

After taking my vitals, the nurse leaves and explains that the doctor will be right with us. We don't have to wait too long before Dr. Robinson walks in. She smiles when she sees me,

"Hi, Gabi, it's good to see you."

"Hi, Dr. Robinson, I hope you don't mind but I brought my boyfriend, Jake McAdams, with me today."

"No problem at all as long as I have your consent to cover your tests results in Jake's presence."

"You have my approval. I'm just going to tell him, anyway. You have my permission to go over the results with him here."

"Before we get down to it, how was your cruise?"

I blush. Why do I blush? She can't tell that Jake takes great care of me in the sex department. Before him, I was on an almost three-year sex hiatus. Well, he has single-handedly addressed my drought repeatedly. "The cruise was great. Jake and I actually met on the cruise."

"I'm happy for you. Now, let's get down to business. I won't keep you in suspense. The ECG ruled out several conditions. The echocardiogram was inconclusive though. I'd like to order a stress test next, but I'd like you to have the test performed this week. The Heart Lab offers extended hours this Wednesday. They normally keep a few open slots for my patients. Can you fit the test into your schedule this week?"

I look over at Jake. He knows why without me having to say anything. Sam will still be out of town, and this would mean that he'd need to stay in Austin for a few more days when he was planning to be in Houston tomorrow. He squeezes my hand and says, "Gabi, don't worry. We can make it work. I'll still be in town."

"Dr. Robinson, I'll get the test this Wednesday."

"Great, it was great seeing you. Since you'll be able to get your test this Wednesday, I'd like to see you back on Friday or Saturday. If Saturday clinic works better, let the nurse know."

"Thanks, Dr. Robinson."

Jake gave me the strength that I needed to focus on Dr. Robinson. I trust her opinion and have confidence that any additional test is not just a throw-everything-against-the-wall-and-see-what-sticks exercise. I release a deep breath that I didn't even realize that I was holding.

"Are you okay?"

I'm not sure. Am I okay? Not the bad news I was expecting but I still have another test to do. I'll get the stress test then see what's next. I look up and notice concern etched across Jake's face. This man, he loves me unconditionally. I move closer and give him a quick kiss before answering, "I think I am. I'm disappointed having to take another test, but on the bright side, we should know the next steps by Saturday."

Jake

My heart skips a beat when I hear her say "we." I will be here every step of the way. I'm not going anywhere. She's my soulmate, my love, my life partner. We'll face challenges together. I don't think that she needs to run back to work since we had the last appointment of the day and it's now after five thirty. "I'm assuming that you don't have to go back to work since it's going on six. Would you like to grab dinner, or I could pick up dinner while you head home since we're in separate cars?"

"Jake, would you mind if we just have pizza tonight? I was so worried about the test results that I'm not hungry. I'd like to watch a show, soak in the tub and head to bed."

"Sounds perfect to me."

The nurse returned with the time slot for the appointment. The sixty-thirty time slot was the only one left for Wednesday. They gave Gabi two options for the follow-up with Dr. Robinson. Gabi took the Saturday morning time slot.

I lace my fingers with hers as we leave the doctor's office. My worry has been for Gabi, and I will take care of her. She's more worried than stressed, but the toll is the same. I'll make sure that she rests when we get home.

AFTER EATING OUR PIZZA, I notice that Gabi only ate one slice and barely touched her side salad. I can tell she has a lot on her mind after today's appointment. My goal tonight is to just be here for her. We head to her bathroom, where I fill the tub with her lavender bubble bath. I turn once the water temperature is just right and say, "Let me." I take off her suit jacket, then unbutton her blouse and slacks. "Do you mind if I join you?"

"Jake, you don't have to. I mean..." I stop her before she can continue.

"I want to. Let me take care of you." She nods.

She sits in the tub but leaves room for me to sit behind her.

I strip and step into the tub as Gabi leans back once I settle behind her. Her garden tub accommodates both of us. Being a big guy, I appreciate the extra room.

I'm resting my right arm on the side of the tub while absently tracing my fingers up and down her left arm. This comfort is for her, but I'm finding just being able to have this quiet time with her gives me peace as well.

I'd be lying if I said that the unknown doesn't scares me. Whatever Gabi's diagnosis is, we'll face it together. My tendency is to take over and fix the problem, but this is outside of our control. Gabi doesn't need me to go all alpha male on her. If I did, it would be out of my love and concern for her, but I need to keep that shit under wraps. She needs me to be here as her support, and that's exactly what I'm going to do.

Gabi

Today has been a lot... I hoped that Dr. Robinson would have said, "the results showed no concerns, see you next year." Though leaning against Jake's muscular, solid chest with his six pack to boot as he strokes my arm soothes me into finding my happy place. "Jake, you've got to know that you're spoiling me–right?" I turn my head to kiss his bicep. Before I settle back, I see his bicep flex and laugh... he's too much. "Did you just flex your bicep?"

"Hey, what can I say? My girl likes my muscles and I aim to please."

When he responds like that, I can't do anything else but shake my head and say, "You're something else, Mr. McAdams."

CHAPTER 9

G^{abi} I've daydreamed throughout the week about Monday night. After our bath, Jake told me to lie down in the bed. I had my eyes closed, so I didn't see when he returned with some warm lavender massage oil. He gave me the best massage that I've ever received. It was so good that I fell asleep and didn't move once the entire night.

Jake moved around his schedule so that he could work from the Austin office. We're back in the waiting room waiting to be called by the nurse so Dr. Robinson can review the results of the stress test. Jake's holding my hand in two of his when he hears me take in a shaky breath.

He leans over and whispers what he said at our first appointment, "We've got this."

I look into his eyes, but before I can answer, the nurse calls my name. We both stand and follow the nurse.

Dr. Robinson doesn't keep us waiting, "Hi Gabi. Good to see you again. Let's go over the results. The stress test confirmed that you have heart arrhythmia, which is a fancy word for an abnormal heart rhythm."

"Oh... okay. Are you sure? I have had no indication that something is wrong. I feel fine."

"Yes, I'm sure. On the bright side, my point of view is we're catching it early and you appear to have a mild case. I'd recommend additional testing to be sure though."

"What would it mean for me if I'd like to hold off?"

"You can make this choice. I'd want to see you once a year to include running the same tests to confirm that they're not any changes and sooner if you experience any symptoms."

I ask, "What's the test? Can you give us more information? I'd prepared myself for some news but now I... if I'm being honest, I hoped it was nothing at all."

Dr. Robinson explains, "The test pinpoints the arrhythmia and enables us to develop a targeted treatment plan versus trying different therapies."

I look over to ask Jake for his thoughts. "What do you think?"

"Gabi, having the test may give you some peace of mind, but I support whichever option you choose."

"Dr. Robinson, can I think about it?"

"Absolutely. this is a lot to absorb. Take your time. Here's the name of the cardiologist and the name of the test in case you'd like to do your own research. Call my office once you've made your decision. Nurse Nadine will send over the referral to Dr. Rodriguez if you decide to have the test. I'll leave the door open. When you're ready, just follow the exit sign to the lobby."

I'M GOING THROUGH MY normal Sunday evening pampering routine while sitting on my pink barrel vanity and applying my favorite apricot vanilla body butter.

After rubbing the body butter up and down my legs several times, I sit back up and see Jake standing in the doorway with heat in his eyes. He walks slowly towards me, and I'm frozen in place as a shiver runs down my spine. He looks like he wants me in a bad way. Well, he's in luck because I want him... I want him right now.

"Is this what you do every Sunday?" asks Jake in a deep voice that washes over me.

I don't hear what he said... I'm too focused on the concentrated intent swimming in his gaze.

"Gabi?"

"Huh?"

He chuckles deeply, and I'm not even ashamed. "I asked... is this what you do every Sunday?"

I have to lick my lips first before answering. My juices pool between my legs. Apparently, my body recognizes what's coming. "Yes, this is my normal routine."

He steps in front of me and kneels between my legs while saying in a graveled voice, "You don't say."

When he opens me wider so he can fit his broad muscled shoulders, I damn near whimper. He kisses up my right thigh but does not go to my center... no, he's taking his time and torturing me in the process by making me wait. He kisses up my left thigh and finally trails his hand up my other thigh until he's opening me with his fingers. At first, he's slowly stroking up and down while soaking his fingers with my juices. Oh, sweet baby Jesus, he finally sucks my clit while taking two of fingers and stroking me in a rhythm that has me about to come.

He continues his slow torture by revving me up then backing off. By his third round, finally... he puts me out of my misery, gets down to business and begins flicking my clit with his tongue in rapid laps that hurls me off a cliff. My orgasm slams into me, "Jake... ohhhhhhh!!!"

Jake

When I walked into Gabi's bathroom, I didn't think that I'd see the woman I love doing something so sensual. She doesn't even see the beauty that I see lying under the surface. Everything Gabi does is sexy to me but being here to witness this. I'm the man that she chose and will be the man that she deserves.

Her scent drives me out of my fucking mind. I can't get enough. I've already given her orgasm number one and focused on one more when I see Gabi looking at us in the mirror. I'm so hard right now... and just got harder knowing that she's watching us and getting turned on.

After orgasm number two, I stand and help Gabi stand. I turn her so she's facing the mirror, get my condom on in record time, and enter her from behind. With short, fast strokes, my orgasm builds. I want to make this last a little longer. I slow down my pace and stroke her long and hard... long and hard.

I bend and say, "Baby, I'm getting close. I believe you have one more orgasm in you." I stroke Gabi's clit while continue to pump into her with deep strokes.

"Jake. I'm... I'm."

She tightens around me, which triggers my orgasm. I grip her hips while continuing to drive into her. Every time... every time, is better than the last. I need a minute to catch my breath. I lay my head on her shoulder then give her shoulder a kiss, "I promise I didn't come in here to.... to...."

"Make me forget my name," offers Gabi.

I chuckle and say, "Yes, that."

GABI

In between working my insane twelve-to-fourteen-hour days, I've continued to have an internal debate regarding whether to proceed with the electrophysiological testing. After speaking with Jake and Sam, I knew I needed my mom's advice on what to do. My mom listened as I gave her the download of my journey to understand what was going on with my heart. I should have spoken to her first. She shared that we have a family history of heart arrhythmia... boy was I relieved to discover most are mild like mine. In the rare instances where the issue was more pronounced, our family member has been in their late eighties to early nineties.

Now armed with the additional information from mom, I shared my decision with Jake and Sam that I will forego the additional test. They both agreed and confirmed they would have taken the same approach based on the facts.

CHAPTER 10

G abi
    "Gabi, what's wrong? You've been sitting there staring off into space for about five minutes. Is everything ok?" asks Sam.

"Well, I'm not sure. Everything is going well with me and Jake. I'm concerned that I may not recognize if I start to lose myself again now that I'm in a relationship. Jake's great and everything that I've always wanted." She nods as I continue, "Richard and I dated for two years. He was the ideal boyfriend for a while... maybe six months or more. He maintained his best behavior for so long that I think... no, I know I dropped my defenses. I didn't even recognize the constant nit picking when it started happening until towards the end of our relationship where I was looking at photos of us from a gala that we attended. I didn't recognize myself... seeing myself in bland makeup that didn't even match my skin color or how flat my hair looked; believe it or not that wasn't the biggest shocker. I'd lost a lot of weight... you know that I'm normally a size 6/8 but had gotten down to a size 2. The sad part was it wasn't until we broke up that I saw all the subtle ways that Richard picked away and manipulated until I became his ideal woman."

Now that I've started talking, I can't stop. "I mean Sam... you know my parents. They're more in love now than when we were growing up. My dad supports my mom in anything that she wants to do. My mom constantly reminds me he's her biggest cheerleader and encouraged her to take her first consulting gig working on the Houston Mayoral race close to fifteen years ago, where she created data models to assess potential voters and developed campaign strategies. Now, she's the department head for the Political Science department and partners with political strategists all over the world."

"Gabi, I wish I could see the future but getting to know Jake, I don't see him being anything but supportive."

"Well, as usual, you've nailed my issue. I can't see the future. I'm afraid that I could easily get consumed with being with Jake and what it would mean being Mrs. Jake McAdams. I'm concerned about the expectations that come along with being with him. I'm still figuring out who I am and what I want to do with the rest of my life. I want the option to explore, choose, and find my passion. I don't want the choice taken out of my hands. I would hate down the road to feel trapped in a life that I didn't sign-up for." I take a slow sip of wine as I collect my thoughts. "Sam, am I being irrational?"

"No, I don't think that you're irrational and I understand your perspective. I have one question for you though... wouldn't you have the same potential issues with someone else?" She raises her hand stopping me from responding and continues, "I recognize he comes from a prominent family in Houston, but you could end up with a professor who is a department head where you'd need to host countless boring dinners as he courts big money donors to fund his next research. Wouldn't you end up being trapped in a life that you didn't envision for yourself?"

Shit, I hate it when she comes up with a good argument. "I need to think this through, Sam. I hear you... I do. I'm not sure if the expectations of being with Jake versus a college professor are anywhere close to being the same though."

"Fine, you may be right. Let me ask you this, but I don't want you to answer me tonight. Think seriously about this. Would you prefer a life with or without Jake?"

"Mic drop, why don't you. Shit, I hate when you go all Judge Mathis on me... I promise to do some soul searching."

WALKING INTO THE HOUSTON chapter of the Texas Society of Architects fundraiser, I notice that Jake's family's firm is a major sponsor. Everyone has been nice and welcoming, as Jake has introduced me to his friends and colleagues. Looking around at the women attending with their significant others, they are wearing pale colors, pearls, and low heels with their hair up in a bun. As I sip my champagne, awareness slams into me, making me lose my breath. I look down and realize that I'm a carbon copy of these women. How did I let this happen? My fear of losing myself... of losing my identity is staring me in the face.

I promised myself that I would never let this happen again after Richard and his controlling, manipulative ways. His suggestions started innocent enough... "wear low-heel shoes since I'm not sure how far we'll have to walk"... only to arrive and there was valet parking. I'm convinced that he knew all along we wouldn't need to walk a long distance.

I need space... I need air. I blindly walk through the crowd until I see open doors leading out to a balcony. My legs tremble as I walk to the opposite corner from the couple who are in a heated debate. Placing my hand on my stomach, I try to breathe... try to catch my breath. Shit, shit, shit, how the hell did I let this happen. What am I going to do?

My commitment to myself doesn't include becoming a shell of the woman that I am, especially for a man. I should have known this was what Jake wanted. How I look today, I'll fit right into his life and portray the perfect partner. I know me... this will not work. After leaving Richard, my friends shared it was like having to un-brainwash me. My laugh sounded forced for over a year after the breakup. I thought I sounded like someone who was having a great time with my newfound freedom. I fooled some of my friends, but not Sam... never Sam. She didn't give up on me but helped me find me again.

A familiar touch rests on my waist as Jake says, "There you are."

I blink rapidly to remove the tears pooling in my eyes before turning to face Jake. He takes one look at me and says, "Gabi, what is it? Is everything ok?"

"No, Jake. I'm not ok. I can't stay. You haven't been here long. I don't mind ordering a ride back to the hotel."

"Gabi, I'd feel much better if I take you. Let me take you back."

Jake

I've looked over at Gabi periodically as I'm driving back to the hotel. She's quiet, looking out the window and only answering with a 'yes' or 'no' as I try to figure out what's wrong. She was fine getting ready for the event and as I introduced her to my colleagues, so what happened.

Once we're in our hotel room, I take off my tie. Watch Gabi as she walks over to the couch in the living room of the suite. "Gabi, I can tell something is wrong. What is it, baby? You know you can tell me anything."

"Jake, I... I can tell that this will not work. It's best that we just end our relationship now before this goes any further."

"What is it? Is it something that I did? If it is, let me fix it. I know I can fix it."

"I'm sorry Jake. I disagree. I don't think that you can. I realize that even though I love you, I'm losing who I am in this relationship."

"What do you mean?"

"I'm not sure if I can explain it so you understand my point of view."

"Try me, Gabi. For the love of all things that are holy, tell me what you're talking about."

"Today's function gave me a glimpse into our life together and the cost to me trying to fit into your world."

"I only want you. I don't have any expectations that you need to be anyone other than who you are."

"Jake, you say that, but that's not how the real-world works. I would never want to embarrass you, but I don't see how I can be true to myself and fit into your world. Today was a perfect example where I noticed that, either consciously or subconsciously, I stripped away every semblance of my true self. I can't dim who am I to be with you. I did it once before with Richard and won't ever allow it to happen to me again."

"I only want you. I'm not asking you to be anyone else than who you are. I love you, Gabi. Just the way you are, can't you see that?"

"You're a great guy, Jake. I'm trying to do the right thing here."

"For who?"

"I'm sorry Jake. I need some space right now."

"Gabi, I don't want to breakup so if space is what you need. I'll give it to you."

I turn and do the hardest thing that I've ever done... I walk towards the door. I look Gabi in her eyes and say with conviction, "Gabi, remember that I love you. I love you with all my heart." I almost forget that we're in a hotel. "Don't worry about checking out. I'll come back to grab my things. If you need a ride to the airport, let me know." I walk out and close the door behind me with a soft click leaving my heart in the hotel room.

Mindlessly, I walk through the lobby and stop at the bar. After ordering a drink, I replay everything starting back to this morning. We ordered room service, enjoyed breakfast and caught up on our week apart. We made love before dressing for the function and arrived in time to hear the keynote speaker. Everyone enjoyed meeting Gabi and engaged her in conversation. So, what happened between me leaving to grab her another glass of champagne and her hiding away on the balcony?

Long-distance relationships aren't easy. We've gotten into a rhythm though of seeing each other every weekend while speaking every evening before heading to bed. I'm usually the one going to see her, but it doesn't bother me. I like the drive, prefer that I'm the one on the road, and can work from Austin occasionally.

I'm racking my brain trying to understand her concern that I want to change her. I would never want to change her. One thing that I love about Gabi is her essence. Gabi's vibrance spills over into everything that makes her unique... her inner light shines bright, her optimism contagious. I'm a moth to her flame. Now, how the hell do I convince her I want her just the way she is?

I promised that I'd give her some space. It may kill me, but I will... I'll give her the space that she needs.

WEEK TWO WITHOUT GABI... I'm not sleeping; I'm barely going through the motions of eating. Immersing myself in work by working insane hours seems to be the only thing that numbs my pain. CJ and Travis continued to try getting me to join them at a bar after work for the past week. To get them off my back, I finally said "yes."

I see CJ and Travis in a corner standing next to a bar top table as I walk into the bar. Perfect timing, the server just brought our beers. No surprise, we ease into our normal topics... sports, our upcoming triathlon and work. After returning from the bathroom, I jokingly say, "So, what is this? Is this an intervention?"

CJ looks at Travis. Travis looks at CJ. Looks like CJ pulled the short straw because he speaks. "We're worried about you, man. You look like you're getting very little sleep."

"I'm working through this the best way that I know how. She wanted space. I'm trying to keep my word by giving it to her."

"Would it help to go through what happened on the day of the Society function again? Are you sure that there wasn't something that you said or did?"

"I've been racking my brain. Nothing stands out. We had a relaxing morning leading up to the function. I'd taken her around to meet a few of my colleagues. Everyone welcomed her, and she even clicked with a few of the significant others. I left to refill her champagne but couldn't find her when I returned. After looking for five minutes, I found her outside on the balcony." A memory crashes into me. She looked freaked out... like a deer caught in headlights freaked out. "I just remembered something. When I found her, I could tell that she was on the verge of tears, and she looked like she was ready to bolt."

CJ nods his head. "Ok, we're getting somewhere. Was there anything else?"

"No, nothing else stands out."

CJ asks, "Tell me exactly what she said when you got back to the hotel."

I take a moment to collect my thoughts. It's like watching a movie in slow frames... the scene ingrained in my memory. I'm having an out-of-body experience as I talk, even my voice sounds hollow, "she said something about going to the function with me, gave her a glimpse into our life together. The cost to her of having to fit into my world."

CJ latches on to this. "Those were her exact words?"

"Yes, that's what she said. Does it make sense to you?"

CJ nods, "I think it does. Don't take this the wrong way, but it's a black thing so you may not understand."

Anger barrels through me... I'm barely hanging on by a thread when I speak through clenched teeth, "What the hell is that supposed to mean? Damn man, just give it to me straight."

"Ok, you've said that Gabi comes from an affluent family - like her mom is a professor and created a consulting firm working with political candidates all over the world, plus her godfather earned a Nobel Peace Prize, right?"

"Yes, what does this have to do with any of this?"

"For black folks, our type of affluent differs from a white person's affluent, then pile on y'all being an interracial couple trying to exist in each other's world. This was the first time where you've come out of your bubble. Am I right? My theory is this may be part of the reason that freaked her out."

I agree with CJ, "You may be onto something."

"Give her the time that you promised. I'm betting that she'll come around," says CJ.

I look at both of them. We were young when we became friends but are now men. I wouldn't want to go through this with anyone else. "Thanks man. I appreciate you both just being here for me."

CHAPTER 11

Gabi

I'm not sleeping, not eating, and if I'm honest, I miss Jake. Sam has given me space to unpack my concerns, but just called to let me know that she's bringing over our favorite sushi and wine.

There's a saying that perception is reality. Well, I don't know if I ever realized exactly what it means until this week. To get out of my head, I resorted to drawing a line down the middle of a piece of paper, putting Jake's name on one side and Richard's on the other side. No surprise, the list on Richard's side was long on all the ways he manipulated me to be the vision of the woman he wanted by his side. Except for the Society event, Jake's side was more about what could happen, not what had happened.

Before I can complete my thought, my doorbell rings. I look through the peephole and open the door. "Hey, Sam."

"Hey, yourself." She looks me up and down. I'm woman enough to know that I look horrendous with not washing off my makeup from work yesterday, nor combing my hair.

I raise my hand to my head to smooth down all the areas where my hair sticks up all over my head. I'm about to defend my appearance when Sam raises her hand, shakes her head, and says, "Let's eat. We have plenty of time to talk."

I love Sam. She never judges. I swear she knows me better than I know myself. We've eaten and starting on our second glass of wine when I start, "You know I asked Jake for some space."

"Yes, I do. Now you know why I'm here. I want to be a sounding board or just to listen... whatever you need as you sort it out."

"You're probably the only person who knows the damage that Richard did to me. If he hadn't broken it off, I'm afraid where I would have ended up. I'm pretty sure that I would have married him and be in a loveless marriage by now."

"Horrible doesn't come close to describing Richard. For the record, I never liked him. He was controlling, condescending, arrogant, and those were his good traits. When he consumed all of your time and drove a wedge between us, I knew he was up to no good."

"Until we broke up, I hadn't realized that I spent all my time with Richard or Richard and his friends. You and I kept in touch, but barely. Over time, he continued to recommend subtle changes to my hair and wardrobe that I didn't realize it when it was happening nor recognized myself afterwards. Do you know he told me wearing my hair naturally curly was too ethnic?"

"Too ethnic? You've got to be kidding me, Gabi. He was black, or did he forget?"

"I still don't know why I went along. Why didn't I speak up for myself? I never want to make that mistake again. Unfortunately, truth be told, maybe I didn't trust myself enough not to make the same mistake twice and avoided dating over the past three years."

"I hear you Gabi. I truly do. Can I ask just two questions?" I nod so she proceeds, "Has Jake ever done anything to make you think he doesn't love you for who you are or tried to change you in any way?"

"You know, if you'd asked me these questions last week, I would have said that I don't know. I took the time to do a side-by-side comparison, so I know the answers. Jake's only crime, loving me unconditionally. I think I freaked out when I noticed I was a carbon copy of the other women at the event. I still don't know if I channeled the selections that I made from hair to makeup to the outfit." I look down, shake my head as a tear drops. When I look back up at Sam, I say,

"Sam, I miss Jake something awful. I made a mistake, but I don't know how to get him back."

"You may not agree, but I think you should call and tell him you'd like to come over. Didn't you mention that you have Monday off work?"

"I do. What if he doesn't want to talk to me?"

"Girl please, that man loves you. Give him a chance. My bet is on Jake... he just might surprise you."

AFTER SPEAKING WITH Jake last night, I got a good night's sleep and drove to Houston first thing this morning. Butterflies flutter in my stomach like the daily butterfly release at Moody Gardens in Galveston. I swear that there must be about a hundred butterflies fluttering around inside me and increase in speed as I park in front of Jake's condo. Every time that I tried to practice my speech, I'd lose my train of thought. Well, here goes nothing... I'm just going to speak from the heart. I knock and am about to knock again when Jake opens the door. I'm at a loss for words as I greedily take him in from head to toe. I thought at one point I would never see him again.

"Hi, Jake. Is now a good time?"

Jake steps aside without saying a word and lets me walk into his living room.

I don't know why I feel awkward. I finally ask, "Do you mind if I sit?"

"Please, do. Gabi, would you like anything to drink... water, soda, wine?"

"Maybe some water?"

"Sure, I'll be right back."

I take a few sips water before I start. "Jake, I owe you a huge apology. I freaked out the day of the event and I wanted to say that I'm sorry."

"I've played that day over and over in my mind, but never could pinpoint what happened. After speaking with Travis and CJ, I think that I have an idea, but can you explain? I'd really like to understand."

"As you know, I hadn't been in a relationship for almost three years before we met. One reason, my last boyfriend relentlessly emotionally abused me. He constantly berated how I dressed, how I wore my hair... hating my natural curly hair, and how I carried myself. At first, his suggestions were subtle. I didn't even realize how much I'd changed myself for him until he'd broken up with me. I promised myself that I'd never allow myself to fall prey to that again and to end a relationship as soon as I saw any hint of those same signs."

"My god, Gabi. I have a sister. I'd never treat a woman like that. Did I do those things to you?"

"No, Jake. You haven't, but here's the thing. When we went to the event, I looked around and noticed that I dressed like the other women. We were all wearing pale colors, pearls, very little makeup... in a nutshell, very conservative. I had an 'oh shit' moment and freaked out. I'd convinced myself that there had to be something that you said or hinted at that drove my choices. I realize now that you did nothing wrong. It was a crazy coincidence."

"Gabi, I wish that you'd shared your fears with me, but I understand. I love *you*. You know that I only want you. I don't want a watered-down version of you. I remember when you first caught my eye on the cruise. You drew me right in. I've always been able to just be myself with you. I want the same for you. I love you unconditionally."

Jake

I look up to see tears streaming down Gabi's face. "Oh, baby, please don't cry. Is it something that I said?" She nods, "What was it?"

"You still love me. I was afraid that you didn't love me anymore."

"I never stopped. Giving you the space that you needed damn near killed me. I wanted to call or drive to see you so many times."

"I love you too, Jake."

I pull her into my arms as she continues to cry. I pull back and wipe her tears with my thumb while realizing how close I came to losing the love of my life. Shit... I'm rocked to my core with this reality and trying to hold back my tears. I can't wait another minute. I kiss each of her eyelids, then the tip of her nose before kissing her on the lips. I pull Gabi onto my lap as we continue to kiss. Kissing her is like basking in the sun on a beautiful Texas Spring Day.

I lift Gabi in my arms and head to my bedroom. We make love all night long. I'm ready to put a ring on it but I know we need more time together as a couple and I need to ask Gabi's dad for her hand in marriage. All in due time... all in due time.

EPILOGUE

Gabi
  Six Months Later

By the time I realized that not only did I want to spend the rest of my life with Jake, I wanted to marry him without wasting another moment. The only thing that held me back from eloping was my mom. Not being able to plan her only daughter's wedding would have been a disappointment. Jake's mom wanted to help plan the wedding as well.

By planning the wedding together over the past six months, they've developed a close bond. They call each other all the time, get mani/pedis together, and take the occasional craft class when they can fit one in.

No surprise... with us having the wedding in Houston, our moms struggled to keep the guest list under two hundred. The wedding planner pulled some strings so we could have our reception at The Corinthian wedding venue. I absolutely fell in love with the ballroom and grand staircase. The flower arrangements throughout are low-profile centerpieces with pink roses and white hydrangeas. I chuckle at the memory of the wrong bouquet being delivered to my room during the cruise with the pink roses (our private secret). Now that the DJ announced the first dance, they have dimmed the lights with a light pink lighting on the fourteen floor-to-ceiling columns that surround the dance floor.

Jake pulls me into his arms as *Spend My Life with You* by Eric Benet and Tamia plays.

"Have I told you how beautiful you are, Mrs. McAdams?"

"You have... you're just saying that because you think that you're going to get lucky tonight," I tease.

Jake pulls me even tighter as he whispers, "I can't wait until I'm making love to my wife. I plan to love you all night long."

I shiver and smile as I hear the tinkling of glasses. I bet Jacqui leads this round. I caught her earlier after the toasts. Jake doesn't disappoint. He leans down and kisses me briefly. I follow his lips as he pulls away and blush. He can make me forget where I am with just a touch, a kiss or a look. "I love you, Jake."

"I love you, too, Gabi, but I must warn you... if you keep looking at me like you're ready to get me naked, too, we'll disappear, have our own private party while everyone continues to party down here without us."

"As much as I want to do just that... you know both of our moms would kill us. I must warn you that my cousins would never let us live it down and Jake, you're just really getting to know everyone. In my family, once you do anything embarrassing or memorable, they will never let you forget it. They'll wait to the perfect time to recount the memory to get the biggest impact, like waiting for a large family gathering when there's a lull in the conversation so a majority of the family hears it and can take part in piling on."

Jake laughs, "I can't wait."

Jake

With the normal wedding stuff behind us now, I can tell that Gabi is really enjoying herself. She's talking with Sam, Jacqui, and a few of her friends from college. Jacqui says something that makes her laugh and my heart beats a little harder. I love my wife with everything that I am. While planning to move to Austin, Gabi shared that she'd prefer that we made Houston our home. We both want to start a family after our first year of marriage and Gabi wants to be near her family and mine, so our children will have a close relationship with their grandparents. This makes me happy because it makes her happy.

FOR YOU TO LOVE

When Gabi submitted her resignation, her boss refused to accept it. He counteroffered with a work from home opportunity from Houston. She accepted the offer but only if she could take four weeks off... that's my girl.

We've been looking for a house for the past three months and found a five-bedroom-four-bath Mediterranean-style house in the affluent River Oaks subdivision that Gabi had her heart set on two months ago. Unfortunately, the seller chose a different offer. Our realtor informed me this morning that the other buyer had to back out because of having to a take a long-term assignment overseas. We still need to live in my condo for a month or two when we return from our honeymoon, but I consider this a small price to pay to live in our dream house. I can't wait to share the good news with Gabi.

Just when I'm about to turn, a tight grip grabs on my left shoulder as CJ hands me a glass of bourbon and says, "Congrats, man. We're happy for you." I smile and am just about to give him a hard time about disappearing with Sam. I should give him shit since I notice the lipstick on his collar looks like the same shade that Sam is wearing. Gabi finally shared the details of what went down between Sam and Derek, that guy that Sam met on the cruise. I say 'good riddance'. She deserves a good guy like CJ.

After raising his glass, CJ says, "Here's to the happy couple," and Travis adds, "I'm surprised you could wait this long to marry your girl. CJ, you should have seen him on the cruise when he'd just met Gabi. He was ready to get down on one knee then, but all kidding aside, I'm happy for you, man. Gabi makes a beautiful bride."

CJ, Travis and I have been through many life challenges together. They have my back, and they know that I have theirs–anytime, anyplace, anywhere. I haven't shared the news about the house with them because I want to tell Gabi first. They knew how much we really wanted that house.

I turn back to see Gabi dancing with her friends, "I'm one lucky bastard, that's all I know."

"How much longer before you steal your bride away? Me and the fellas have a wager going," says CJ.

"Damn, really man? Well, it probably doesn't help my cause, but I've been ready since she walked down the aisle."

CJ and Travis both laugh then say, "I bet."

CJ states, "You need to let me know how you like Sardinia, Italy. I hear this time of year makes a perfect time to visit."

"No promises. Remember... honeymoon. We have a private villa with its own beach, infinity pool, and staff. I really doubt that we're going to see much of the village."

"Well, at least you can tell me what the city looks like from the drive to the villa and the airport amenities," he adds with a chuckle.

"Now that I can do," I laugh and look over at Gabi as I plan when and how to make our exit. If I had to guess, this group looks like they're ready to party into the night. Our moms have thought of everything to include booking the venue past midnight and securing taxis for anyone who may need to be driven home.

Gabi

Jake kept his promise of loving me all night long, multiple times. We couldn't get enough of each other... over... and over again. Each time more intense than the last time. We fell asleep finally before the sun rose. I smile when Jake kisses my shoulder, "why am I not surprised that you're already up."

He pulls me closer to him. He's not the only one who is up, which he confirms by saying, "I'm always up for you."

I love his playful side. When I mentioned this to Jacqui one day, she shared Jake is normally serious and loved that I could bring out something in him she hadn't seen since they were kids.

"All kidding aside, I've been waiting for you to wake up. After we eat, I have a surprise before we head to the airport," says Jake.

JAKE HASN'T GIVEN ME a clue about the surprise. We've been driving for about twenty minutes when he turns into River Oaks subdivision. I wonder if the realtor found another house for us. She knew that I really liked this area. I'll be open, but I've been having a hard time letting go of the Mediterranean-style house that captured my heart.

With Jake keeping me up most of the night, I'm half paying attention. I'm pretty sure that I've dozed off at least once or twice. He stops the car in front of the house where I could see building our life and raising our kids. "Jake, is this the surprise?"

Jake has turned to look at me from the driver's side and say, "Yes, the deal with the other buyer fell through. It's ours if we want it."

I launch myself into his arms and begin kissing his face, jaw, then mouth. I'm jumping up and down in my seat. I'm beyond happy, "Oh my God, Jake. Don't play with me. Is this house really ours if we want it?"

"I wouldn't play with you about this. The realtor called yesterday and said the seller accepted our offer. Want to go inside and sign a few papers?"

I say "Yes," as I run out of the car. This man... I love him and can't wait to build our life together.

Want to read how Gabi and Jake's story began? Read *Could This Be Love*

Books by CD Giles

A Love Blossoms Series Novel
   Could This Be Love, Book #1

For You to Love, Book #2

Next Book in Series
Jacqui and Travis, Book #3
Samantha and CJ, Book #4

Don't miss out!

Visit the website below and you can sign up to receive emails whenever CD Giles publishes a new book. There's no charge and no obligation.

https://books2read.com/r/B-A-BNJU-HNTZB

BOOKS 2 READ

Connecting independent readers to independent writers.

About the Author

Living in the Texas Hill Country with her husband of nearly twenty years, CD Giles is a romantic at heart. Her storybook reunion with her sweetheart began in junior high school. After twenty-two years of bad timing and missed opportunities, the stars finally aligned during a group trip together as adults. They've been together ever since their official first date. C.D. loves a good happily-ever-after story--after all, she's living one! When she's not penning one herself, she's watching rom-coms and spending time with family.

Website: www.cdgiles.com

Instagram: https://instagram.com/cdgilesauthor/

Read more at https://cdgiles.com/.